Europe

Asia

Africa

Australasia

AROUND
THE
WORLD
IN
80
TALES

FOR PAM AND PHIL FLUKE – S. P.
FOR SUSAN, WITH LOVE – R. J.

KINGFISHER
An imprint of Kingfisher Publications Plc
New Penderel House, 283–288 High Holborn
London WC1V 7HZ
www.kingfisherpub.com

First published by Kingfisher 2007
2 4 6 8 10 9 7 5 3 1

Text copyright © Saviour Pirotta 2007
Illustrations copyright © Richard Johnson 2007
The moral right of the author and illustrator has been asserted.
Edited by Jane Casey
Designed by Eliz Hüseyin

A CIP catalogue record for this book is available from the British Library.

ISBN: 978 0 7534 1602 0

Printed in China
1LIB/0707/LFG/CJCL4/140MA/C

AROUND
THE
WORLD
IN
80
TALES

Saviour Pirotta

Illustrated by
Richard Johnson

KINGFISHER

Contents

North America

South America

Europe

Africa

Asia

Australasia

North America

The More the Merrier

A STORY FROM THE USA

A boy named Jack set out to make his fortune, with nothing but a whistle in his pocket. On the road, he met a tabby cat, washing her whiskers.

"Where are you going, Jack?" she mewed.

"To make my fortune."

"How are you going to do that?"

"Come along and find out!" Jack laughed.

The cat joined Jack and on they went together.

Outside a farm they saw a dog burying a bone.

"Where are you two going?"

"To make our fortune."

"How are you going to do that?"

"Come along and find out!"

"I've always wanted to go on an adventure," said the dog. And on he went, along with the cat and Jack the lad. At a crossroads they met a goat, tied to a tree.

"Where are you three going?"

"To make our fortune."

"And how are you going to do that?"

"Come with us and find out!"

Jack untied the goat and on they went — the goat, the dog, the cat and Jack the lad.

At teatime they came across a bull raking the ground with his front leg. "Where are you four going?" he rumbled.

"To make our fortune."

"And how are you going to do that?"

"Come with us and find out!"

"Don't mind if I do!" And on they went together — the bull, the goat, the dog, the cat and Jack the lad.

They passed an oak tree and there was a skunk, peeping round the trunk.

"Where are you five going?"

"To make our fortune."

"And how are you going to do that?"

"Come with us and find out!"

"How nice of you to ask!" And on they went together — the skunk, the bull, the goat, the dog, the cat and Jack the lad.

Soon they came to a hen-house where a rooster was digging around in the dirt, looking for worms.

"Where are you six going?"

"To make our fortune."

"And how are you going to do that?"

"Join us and find out!"

The rooster gobbled one last worm and on they went together — the rooster, the skunk, the bull, the goat, the dog, the cat and Jack the lad.

That night they came across a house in the woods. They peeped in through the window and saw a gang of thieves sitting round a table, counting gold.

"Hide, quick," whispered Jack, "and when I give the signal, make as much noise as you can."

The animals hid in the bushes around the house. When Jack blew his whistle the cat started meowing, the dog started barking, the goat started bleating, the bull started bellowing, the skunk started hissing and the rooster started crowing. The robbers thought the police had arrived, and they fled, leaving the gold behind.

Jack and the animals went inside.

"This is a nice place to spend the night," said Jack. He told the bull to sleep in the cellar, the goat at the top of the stairs, the rooster on the roof, the skunk in the fireplace, the cat in the rocking chair and the dog under the kitchen table. He tucked himself up in one of the beds upstairs.

In the middle of the night, one of the robbers sneaked back to get his gold. The house was very dark and still. He tried to light the fire, so that he could see what he was doing, but when he bent down to the grate, something dirty and smelly squirted into his eye. What was that?

The robber staggered back into the rocking chair and ten sharp claws gouged his behind. He rushed upstairs, howling, but something butted him in the nose and he ran down again. The poor robber didn't know what was happening. He tried to hide in the cellar, but at the bottom of the stairs something hit him in the chest and sent him flying back up.

I'll just grab some of the gold and get out of here, thought the robber. He ran to the table, but something under it growled and sank its teeth into his leg. Now the poor robber could hardly walk. As he stumbled down the porch steps a shadow flew down from the roof, screeching, and something wet landed on his head! Ugh!

"You can keep the gold!" wailed the robber, hobbling into the woods as quickly as he could go. He was sure he had been attacked by a ghost. What else could be in so many places at once?

"I don't think he'll be back," Jack said, chuckling. He scooped the gold up in a sack and off they went to enjoy their fortune — the rooster, the skunk, the bull, the goat, the dog, the cat and Jack the lad, who now had much, much more than a whistle!

The White Bear

A STORY FROM CANADA

The brave hunter Taliriktug had been running for many miles across the ice, chasing a swift caribou. He was exhausted! As he paused for breath, he heard a loud cracking noise under his feet. The ice he was standing on was breaking away from the land. Before he could react, the gap between him and the land was too big to jump. Taliriktug was swept out to sea, where the cold grey waves lapped around his tiny ice-floe.

By nightfall, Taliriktug was hungry and freezing cold. No one had seen him waving or heard him calling for help. He couldn't even catch any fish, as he had dropped his spear in the water.

Taliriktug thought about swimming for land, but he knew he wouldn't last long in the freezing water. "If I dive in," he said to himself, "the sea goddess Sedna will take me by the hair and drag me down to her kingdom at the bottom of the sea."

He settled down to wait for someone to rescue him, huddled in his furs. For days, he drifted further and further away from land.

One night, as he lay shivering on the ice, he thought he saw a huge white bear looking up at

him from the grey waters. "I will help you," it said.

A talking bear? Taliriktug wondered if he had passed over to the land of the dead, so that now he could see wonders that were kept from the living.

The ice-floe swayed as the bear clambered onto it. "Eat," it said, dropping fish in front of the hunter. "You must keep up your strength until you are discovered."

Taliriktug stuffed the raw fish into his mouth, chewing on guts and scales and tails. Perhaps he was not dead after all — the dead don't eat. The bear stretched out on the ice. "Let me wrap my arms around you."

Little by little, the warmth from the bear's pelt melted the ice in the hunter's clothes. The warmth crept into his bones and he fell asleep.

He woke to find the bear's warm tongue licking his face. "Wake up. We are near land."

The hunter stumbled to his feet, peering through the dark.

"The current changed while you were sleeping. You are saved," said the bear. "My work is done."

The ice-floe rocked once more under the bear's weight as it slid back into the sea.

"Have you a name?" Taliriktug asked. "How shall I repay you?"

"I am Nanook the great spirit, helper of man." And with that, the great white bear disappeared beneath the waves.

Taliriktug felt the ice-floe touch land. He leapt off and started walking towards home. Wait until he told his family the whole strange story!

"But did it really happen?" his eldest child asked once he had finished describing what had occurred. "Was the bear a dream, or was it really Nanook who helped you?"

Taliriktug shook his head. "It was no dream. Look what I found on the ice-floe after the bear disappeared." And from his pocket he took a clump of white polar-bear fur, twisted into a knot no one had seen before — a gift from Nanook himself, to prove it was really him who had helped the hunter.

The Three Spells

A STORY FROM THE SIOUX OF THE DAKOTA PLAINS

A brave buffalo hunter called Odakota fell in love with Ehawee, a beautiful maiden.

"Will you marry me?" he asked.

Ehawee shook her head sadly. "Alas, I am the only family my grandmother has left. She will never let me be married."

"I will talk to her," said Odakota.

Ehawee's eyes filled with tears. "She knows many powerful magic spells. If she found out about us, she might put a horrible spell on you."

"Then let us run away tonight," said Odakota. "We will go somewhere that your grandmother cannot reach us."

Late that night Ehawee crept out of her grandmother's lodge in the dark, clutching a bag with her favourite belongings in it. Odakota helped her onto his horse and they stole away across the plain. They hadn't gone very far when Ehawee looked back over her shoulder.

"I fear my grandmother has realized I am gone. She's following us."

"She is too old to catch up with us," laughed Odakota. "Don't worry, we can outrun her."

"She might be ancient," Ehawee replied, "but she has magic boots that make her faster than the wind in a storm. I think I can hear her coming."

The moon came out, and sure enough, there was Granny, stomping across the plain behind them in her magic boots. As they listened, they could hear her calling.

Eha-wee! Eha-wee!
Don't run away from me.

15

"What do we do now?" gasped Odakota, getting worried. "She is gaining on us."

Ehawee had learnt spells from her grandmother over the years. She took off one of her mittens and threw it on the ground. The mitten changed at once into a mad buffalo with pointed horns and a swishing tail. Seeing Granny, it pawed the ground and charged at her.

"That will stop poor Granny in her tracks," laughed Odakota.

But only a short while later, he heard that dreaded voice again, coming from behind them.

Eha-wee! Eha-wee!
Don't run away from me.

Granny had turned the buffalo into an ant, and now she was catching up with them again.

"It's time to use my second spell," said Ehawee. She took a comb from her hair and tossed it into the wind. Instantly the comb turned into a forest, thick with trees and bushes.

"She won't be able to follow us now," laughed Odakota.

But as the sun rose in the sky, the two of them could see Granny fighting her way out of the forest. She struggled through the bushes, cutting the trees down with her walking stick.

Eha-wee! Eha-wee!
Don't run away from me.

"Quickly, Ehawee," Odakota said. "We need another spell."

Ehawee took an awl, a large needle, from her sleeve and threw it over her shoulder. Instantly the awl turned into a range of mountains with jagged peaks and snowy slopes.

"That must put a stop to her," laughed Odakota.

But once again he was wrong. As the sun dipped in the sky, they felt the ground shake and Granny's voice echoed across the plain again.

Eha-wee! Eha-wee!
Don't run away from me.

By now the runaways had come to a river. There was no bridge, and Granny was catching up with them fast. They were trapped.

"What are we to do?" cried Ehawee. "I've run out of spells."

Odakota turned to some cranes that had settled on the bank to drink. "Help us across, my friends, and we shall praise your names forever."

The cranes were pleased by the respectful way the brave hunter had addressed them. They joined up neck to tail, so that they formed a bridge across the river. Ehawee and Odakota hurried across, leaving their horse behind. He would have been too heavy for the cranes.

When they were safely on the other side, they turned to see Granny on the opposite bank, at the water's edge.

"Help me across," she ordered the cranes, "or I'll change you all into lumps of dead wood."

The cranes ruffled their feathers and squawked angrily at the old lady's rudeness. Even so, they joined up again to form a bridge. Granny stomped across their backs — but when she was only halfway across the river, they suddenly spread their wings and flew off. Granny fell into the water, and, with a sizzle and a scream, she melted away into nothing. At last Ehawee was free to marry her beloved Odakota!

The Owl Battle

A STORY FROM HAWAII

This is the story of how Hawaiians came to honour the owl.

Once upon a time, on the island of Oahu, a hungry man named Kapoi climbed up a koa tree to an owl's nest and stole some eggs. While he was wrapping them in leaves, preparing to cook them on the fire, an owl settled in the tree nearby.

"Please do not destroy my eggs, Kapoi," the owl hooted.

The young man's stomach was rumbling with hunger. Why should he give back what he had found unguarded?

"They are mine now," he replied.

"I beg you not to kill my children, Kapoi," said the owl, fluttering its wings.

Kapoi felt ashamed of his selfishness. Suddenly he didn't feel so hungry any more. How could he eat the eggs when the owl was watching him? "Come and take them, then. I cannot have my pleasure at someone else's expense," he said.

The owl settled on his shoulder and whispered, "Thank you, Kapoi. My name is Pueo and I am a god you mortals haven't heard of before. Build me an altar and I shall protect your people from all harm."

A god that pledged to protect people from harm! Kapoi fetched stone and wood and built a small altar. He made a sacrifice to the owl god. The smoke from the altar plumed up into the sky, thanking Pueo for his protection. The owl flew away, hooting softly, and Kapoi knew he had done the right thing.

But someone noticed the smoke in the sky — someone very important. It was the king of Oahu, Kakuhiwewa. "Is someone burning sacrifice without my permission?" he asked crossly. "Don't the people know that only the king may burn sacrifice?"

His guards went out to investigate. "A young man is praying to a new god, the owl Pueo," they reported.

"I do not believe there is such a god," said the king. "Bring the man to me. He must stand trial for lying and disobeying my orders."

An enormous crowd gathered to watch Kapoi's trial.

"You have been worshipping a god we do not recognize," proclaimed the king. "Your sacrifice could make the great goddess of the volcano jealous. She might rain fire on our heads, or even sink our island. I therefore send you into exile, Kapoi. My guards will take you to a deserted island far from home from which you will never return."

A deserted island far from home! It would be an open-air prison, with no one to share music or food with, no one to talk to, no family to visit. "Oh Pueo," whispered Kapoi, "I spared your children's life. Save me from a fate worse than death!"

All at once the sky darkened. Kapoi and the king looked up to see thousands of owls swooping towards them. How strange, when owls usually only came out at night, under the cloak of darkness.

The leader of the guards blew his conch, and the others drew their spears and shark-tooth clubs. The owls descended on them, jabbing with their beaks and talons. The warriors clustered around the king, leaving Kapoi unguarded. One of the owls pecked at the rope around his wrists, freeing him. It was Pueo himself, repaying mercy with mercy.

"The owl is indeed powerful," called King Kakuhiwewa. "We shall build temples and altars in its name. We shall dance for its pleasure."

"And in return, it shall protect us," said Kapoi. "Much glory to Pueo! Much glory to the owl!"

The crowd cheered, and since that day, Hawaiians have always honoured owls.

Anansi and the Plantains

A STORY FROM JAMAICA

Anansi the spiderman had been waiting impatiently for the plantains on his tree to ripen. At last they were ready to pick, but how could he get at them? If he turned into a spider, he would not be able to carry them, but if he remained a man, he could not climb high enough in the tree. What was he to do?

Anansi went to see Horse. "Help me pick my plantains," he wheedled, "and I'll share them with you."

Horse liked plantains! He came at once to Anansi's garden and kicked the tree with his hind legs. Down came the ripe yellow plantains, falling around the spiderman's ears like rain. Anansi rushed around, gathering them up. His mouth was already watering at the thought of eating them.

Anansi gathered wood for a fire. He put a pan on the pile of branches, but didn't light them. "I need some matches, Horse. If you run along and buy some from the market, I'll peel and chop the plantains for when you get back."

But Anansi did more than chop the plantains. He lit the fire with flints, fried the fruit and gobbled up every single one himself. He didn't leave a scrap for Horse.

"I should have known you'd trick me, Anansi," neighed Horse when he came back from the market. "You never

had any intention of sharing your plantains. So I'll never help you again. You'll have to find someone else to pick your fruit." And Horse cantered away, furious with himself for having been tricked by the spiderman.

The next day, Anansi was desperate for more plantains. He could see that some more of the fruit had ripened on his tree, but he still couldn't get at it on his own. What could he do now?

"Hey, Goat," Anansi called. "Help me pick my plantains and I'll share them with you."

Goat loved plantains too. She looked at all the luscious ripe fruit and her mouth watered.

"All right, I'll help you," she said.

She butted the tree with her sturdy horns and down came the fruit, just as it had the day before when Horse had helped Anansi.

"Go and buy matches from the market now, Goat," said Anansi as he piled up the firewood. "I'll get the plantains ready for frying."

"Very well," said Goat, trotting off briskly.

As soon as she was gone, Anansi lit the fire and fried the plantains. How good they smelled — no way was he going to share them with anyone! What a clever trick he had played on Horse and Goat. They had done all the work, and he had got all the delicious plantains!

Anansi sat down to eat, but before he could put a single slice of plantain in his mouth, something hit him in the small of the back and sent him flying into a prickly bush. It was Goat. She'd butted him hard with her sturdy horns, just as she had butted the trunk of the plantain tree. Anansi groaned.

"You thought you'd trick me, Anansi," laughed Goat. "But I saw what you did to Horse yesterday so I didn't go to market when you told me to. I hid behind a tree instead, until the plantains were ready to eat."

Anansi had to sit there, picking prickles out of his skin and rubbing his back, while Goat gobbled up all the plantains, all by herself. If only he hadn't tried to trick her, he could have had some too!

Brer Rabbit Goes Fishing

An African-American story

The afternoon is hot, hot, hot and Brer Rabbit, Brer Fox and some of their friends are digging up a vegetable patch, turning the soil before they plant their seeds. Then that good-for-nothing Brer Rabbit gets fed up with working and sneaks off to find some shade. He comes to a shady, quiet orchard full of leafy peach trees. There, in the middle of the orchard, Brer Rabbit spies a well, with a rusty bucket hanging from a wheel above it. The bucket sways gently in the breeze, like a baby's cradle waiting for a baby.

"That looks like it would be a nice cool place to have a nap," says Brer Rabbit to himself, quite unaware there is a second bucket at the other end of the rope, waiting to come up. He hops into the bucket at the top, and quick as a flash, the rope whizzes around the wheel. Brer Rabbit's weight takes him to the bottom of the well with a splash, sending the empty bucket back up to the top.

"Now, how am I going to get out of this fix?" says Brer Rabbit to himself, feeling a bit squashed in the bucket, cold water lapping all around him.

By and by Brer Fox comes to the orchard, looking for Brer Rabbit. "Where are you, brother? There's more work to be done, you know. We can't start growing those vegetables till the soil's been turned."

A voice floats out of the well. "I am down here, Brother Fox."

"Down the well?" says Brer Fox. "What in charity's name are you doing down there?"

"I am catching fish, Brother Fox," Brer Rabbit calls up from the bottom of the well. "Thought I might cook some for supper."

Brer Fox looks down the well, surprised. He can hardly see Brer Rabbit, the well is so deep. "Are there lots of fish down there?"

"The water's crawling with them. Do you want to catch some too?" Brer Rabbit asks.

Brer Fox's mouth starts to water at the very idea. Fish for supper! What could be more delicious?

"But how can I join you, Brother Rabbit?" he asks, peering into the well. "It looks an awfully long way down."

"There's nothing to it," comes back the reply. "Just get into that bucket up there and it'll bring you down as easy as eel pie."

Brer Fox gets in the bucket, and quick as a flash, starts hurtling towards the bottom of the well. On the way down, he meets Brer Rabbit in his bucket, going up. The wily rabbit is singing:

> Well, Brother Fox, don't wet your toes
> This is how the wicked world goes
> Some go up and some go down
> Never do anything with a frown.

At the top of the well, out of the bucket hops Brer Rabbit, leaving Brer Fox shouting and yelling at the bottom of the well. Brer Rabbit waits a good long time before sending his friends to rescue Brer Fox, and that darned vegetable patch never does get dug that day!

23

The Charcoal-seller's Son

A STORY FROM CUBA

A haughty young contessa stood on her balcony, watching the dancing at a fiesta in the street below. Her toes tapped as she listened to the lively guitar music. Everyone at the fiesta was having lots of fun, but even so, the contessa decided to stay on her balcony. She was an aristocrat, and couldn't mingle with the commoners down below. The contessa smothered a yawn. She was too tired to dance anyway, as she was going to have a baby soon.

While the contessa watched the fun, a poor charcoal-seller spotted her on the balcony. She came to stand on the pavement under the balcony and called up to the contessa, "I notice we are both going to have a baby, my lady. Wouldn't it be wonderful if one of us had a boy and the other a girl? Then our children could marry each other."

The very idea made the contessa wince. A charcoal-seller's child marrying nobility? Whatever next?

Then fear gripped her. What if the charcoal-seller's wish came to pass? The contessa's aristocratic family would be the laughing stock of Cuba.

When her baby, a girl, was born, the contessa sent for her old uncle.

"Find the charcoal-seller. If her child is a boy, kill him and bring me the little finger of his left hand as proof that you have done so."

The uncle went off and returned a day later with a baby's finger in a small wooden box. The contessa smiled a thin, mean smile. *As if a charcoal-seller's son could marry my daughter*, she thought. She had a sign put up on her castle gate:

WHAT GOD GAVE, I TOOK AWAY.

24

As the years passed, the contessa's daughter, Maria, grew into a dazzling, clever young woman. Her beauty was known all over the country, from Havana to Santiago de Cuba. One Sunday she was coming out of church with her mother when a handsome young man on a shiny stallion clattered across the plaza in front of them. He was followed by a train of twenty other men, all dressed in fine clothes.

"Who is that man, Mama?" Maria wondered.

"I don't know," said the contessa, her eyes narrowing as she watched the handsome young man controlling his horse. He did look noble in his fine clothes! Maybe this young man would make a suitable husband for her beautiful daughter.

One of their neighbours overheard their conversation. "He is the governor's son. They say he is travelling across Cuba in search of something."

The governor's son! "We must throw a party for him at once," said the contessa. "Someone, find out where he is lodging so I can invite him."

The very next day, the contessa held a grand ball in her castle. The governor's son danced with Maria all night. He never once took his eyes off her. Nor did he take the glove off his left hand.

Before he left, the governor's son took Maria to one side, knelt before her and asked her, "Will you be my wife?"

"There is nothing in the world I want more," the contessa's daughter replied without a second's hesitation.

"But will you take me for love, or because I am a nobleman?" asked the governor's son.

The answer came in a whisper. "I would marry you even if your mother was a charcoal-seller."

Everyone who was anyone in Cuba attended the wedding, which was held in the grand cathedral. The contessa was proud to welcome the nobility to see her daughter make such a wonderful marriage. As she looked at the rows of guests in the cathedral, there was only one guest the contessa did not recognize. The woman's hunched back and chapped hands suggested she was no noblewoman.

"Who let you in, Señora?" the contessa asked coldly, swishing over to where she was kneeling as soon as the wedding vows were over and the happy couple had been blessed.

"I am a guest of the groom," the stranger replied.

"The groom?" the contessa repeated.

"Why yes," the old woman said, with laughter in her voice. "After all, I am his mother."

She lifted her mantilla, and there was the charcoal-seller, her eyes brimming with triumph.

"My wish, dear Contessa, has come true."

The contessa fell in a dead faint at her feet. All of the doctors in the congregation leapt up and fanned her. When they brought her round, the charcoal-seller explained what had happened. All those years before, the contessa's uncle couldn't kill the charcoal-seller's son. Instead, he cut off the baby's finger and set him loose on the river, like Moses on the Nile. The governor himself had found the rush basket and brought the boy up as his own son. Such a charming young man he turned out to be, and handsome too. He was worthy of his high place in society. When he was old enough, the governor told him he was an adopted child and explained how he had found him on the river. Straightaway, the young man had set out to find his birth mother. He had discovered her in the contessa's town, the day he first met Maria.

"I don't believe it," spat the contessa, her face purple with rage and disappointment.

The groom cleared his throat. "It's true, my lady." He removed his glove to reveal a golden finger on his left hand, and the contessa fainted again. When she came to, Maria and the groom had left for Havana, taking the charcoal-seller with them.

"A charcoal-seller in the family," sobbed the contessa. "Whatever next?" And she had the sign above the castle gate changed to read:

WHAT I TOOK, GOD RETURNED.

The Half-Chick

A STORY FROM PUERTO RICO

Once upon a time, there was a naughty little chick – but what a strange chick he was! He had just one eye, one leg, and one wing. In fact, he was only half a chick. Still, his mother loved him just as much as if he had been a whole chicken. She named him Half-Chick.

Now, Half-Chick longed to see the world. As soon as he was old enough, he said goodbye to his mother and set out on a journey. He was going to visit the walled city of San Juan, because he wanted to meet the governor.

As Half-Chick hopped along, he had to cross a stream. It was the middle of summer and there was only a narrow trickle of water in the stream.

"Please, little half-chicken, help me," murmured the water. "If you move those twigs out of my way, I can flow more freely."

"I haven't got time to help you," chirped Half-Chick, hopping over the trickle. "I'm off to San Juan to see the governor."

Further along the road, Half-Chick heard another voice calling.

"Please, little half-chicken, help me."

Half-Chick sighed impatiently. Not someone else trying to delay him! Who was it now?

"I am the breeze," said the voice, "and I'm caught in the branches of the almond tree behind you. Can you untangle me?"

"That would take hours," said Half-Chick, "and I'm in a hurry to get to San Juan before the sun sets."

He continued hopping along on his one leg and quite soon he could see the walls of the city. Just then, he heard another voice.

"Please, little half-chicken. Help!"

Half-Chick shook his head, trying to block out the noise. Why didn't everyone let him travel in peace? Couldn't they see he was in a hurry? He looked around for the voice's owner.

"Over here," the voice called. "I'm under the farmer's coffee pot."

A little spark was struggling to stay alight between two stones. "The silly farmer went and left me unattended, without any fuel to burn. Can you fetch some twigs to keep me alive?"

"I'm almost in San Juan, I can't stop now," snapped Half-Chick, and he hopped on without once looking back.

In San Juan, Half-Chick wasted no time in locating the governor's palace by the sea. He jumped in through an open window and found himself in the kitchen.

"May I see the governor? I'd really like to meet him. I have important matters to discuss with him," he cheeped.

The cook had been waiting for some chickens to be delivered. He grabbed Half-Chick in his big beefy hands. "You'll see the governor all right. From his plate!"

Poor Half-Chick didn't even have time to protest. The cook wrung his neck and called for a bucket of boiling water so he could dip Half-Chick in it. That would help him to pluck the feathers from the bird before he cooked him.

"Water, water," begged Half-Chick, "please don't scald me."

"You wouldn't help me when I asked you to in the stream," said the water, "so don't ask for mercy now."

The cook put the plucked chick in a dish and popped him in the oven.

"Fire, fire, please don't burn me," begged Half-Chick, who was starting to go brown around the edges.

"You wouldn't help me when I was under the farmer's coffee pot and I needed fuel," said the fire, "so please don't think I'm going to have pity on you," and he roared so loudly around Half-Chick that in no time at all he had burnt him to a crisp.

"What a waste," said the cook, opening the oven and looking at the blackened remains of the bird. He threw the chicken out of the window onto a rubbish heap. As Half-Chick flew through the air, the wind leapt onto him and blew him across the square.

"Oh wind, wind, please put me down," begged Half-Chick desperately.

"I recognize that voice," howled the wind. "You are the half-chicken that walked by when I needed help. Don't worry, I'll put you down, all right." He blew Half-Chick to the top of a nearby church and dropped him on top of the steeple. "How do you like it up there?" the wind said with a laugh.

And Half-Chick stayed where he had been put. It didn't take long for the wind, the rain and the heat of the sun to turn the burnt and blackened chicken into a weathervane. He still stands on top of the church, being teased by the wind, the rain and the heat of the sun — all because he didn't help when he had the chance!

Red Ant, Black Ant

A STORY FROM MEXICO

The young god Quetzalcoatl sat on a rock in the forest and watched a red ant scurrying across the ground, carrying a heavy load. The ants were always busy, gathering food and stowing it away.

Quetzalcoatl sighed. He couldn't help but be worried. The ants would have plenty of food for winter. Humans, on the other hand, might not have much to live on. Quetzalcoatl had only just created them, and for the moment they lived on water and leaves. That was a good way to live in summer, but there was one problem – soon winter would strip the trees bare. Quetzalcoatl knew the people would starve unless he could give them something that would keep them going through the dark season, when nothing grew.

But what could he give them? They needed something to hoard, like the ants.

The red ant scurried back, this time without its burden. Quetzalcoatl wondered what it was doing. Quickly, he changed himself into a black ant and ran after it.

"Where are you going?" he asked.

"To collect food from the Mountain of Riches," the ant replied and hurried on. The black ant followed close behind it. The Mountain of Riches? What kind of riches? Did the red ant mean treasure?

At the foot of the mountain, the red ant squeezed into a little tunnel, a crack in the rock. The black ant panted after it. What a long dark tunnel it was, twisting and turning till it opened out into a cave, right in the middle of the mountain. At the sight of the cave, the black ant gasped in amazement. Here were piles of golden treasure that stretched almost to the roof of the cave. Not diamonds or gold, but seeds of every kind! They had been hidden there by the ancient gods.

The seeds were the perfect answer to Quetzalcoatl's problems. He knew what he had to do at once. He picked up one seed and carried it through the tunnel on his back. Then he went back for another one, and then another one, until he had collected up enough seeds to plant a small field. He could save his humans from suffering during the winter!

Taking the form of a human again, he spoke to the people. "Listen to me," he said. "I bring you a gift from the gods that will help you all."

He showed them the pile of seeds, then told them to bury the seeds in the ground. He explained that they had to water the earth and protect the seeds from hungry birds and insects. The humans learned quickly and looked after the little seedlings carefully. Quetzalcoatl was pleased to see that by the end of the summer, the seeds had grown into tall plants bearing the first ears of corn. His plan was working!

Quetzalcoatl helped the humans to gather the first harvest. Then he taught them how to cook the cobs and grind the kernels into flour to make tortillas. He instructed the elders to store some of the kernels for them to eat during the winter months, and gave them others to put aside for planting in the spring.

The people survived the winter and flourished, planting their seeds in the spring as Quetzalcoatl had shown them. They thanked Quetzalcoatl and blessed his name, and the god smiled to see their happiness. And it was all thanks to the little red ant who showed him the secret of the mountain.

The Golden Horseshoe

A STORY FROM GUATEMALA

Don Pedro was very upset. Every night, wild animals broke into his fields and trampled all over his corn. What was he to do?

"The harvest will be ruined if I can't put a stop to this!" he said to his sons.

"I'll keep watch in the field tonight, Papa," said Manolo, his eldest son. "I'll catch them."

That night, Manolo spread a soft rug on the ground and lay on it while he kept watch. But halfway through the night he fell asleep and the wild animals wreaked havoc in the corn again.

The next night, his brother José tried to keep watch. Like Manolo, he too fell asleep and let the wild animals damage the corn.

"Perhaps Miguel can catch the vandals," said Don Pedro. Manolo and José laughed out loud. Miguel was their youngest brother, a foolish dreamer who thought he would join the circus one day. How could he succeed where they had failed?

Miguel did not spread a rug on the ground. Instead he sat in a high-backed chair and practised twirling a rope to keep awake.

Shortly after midnight, he heard a flurry of wings and six horses landed in the field, neighing and prancing around in the corn. Miguel threw his lasso and captured the one nearest to him. The wild horse reared up on its hind legs but it could not escape with the others.

Miguel tied his prisoner up and sat back to wait for the dawn. In the morning light, he looked at the horse and realized it was very special indeed. Not only did it have wings, but its coat was coloured like a rainbow!

"I am the king of the flying horses," said the beast. "Let me go."

"Only if you promise to leave my father's crops alone," replied Miguel.

"I promise," said the king of the horses and Miguel untied the rope from around its neck.

"Take one of my golden horseshoes as a gift," said the rainbow horse, beating its wings as it rose in the air. "If you ever need help, touch it and I will come."

Now that his father's crops were safe, Miguel put the horseshoe in his satchel and set off to seek his fortune.

By and by he came to a large city where a great king lived. The king's daughter wanted a husband, but she wasn't prepared to wed any ordinary rich count or baron. She wanted to marry someone daring and brave — someone with guts! So the princess had come up with an ingenious idea, a contest. She would stand at the top of the tallest tower in the land, holding a wedding ring. She would marry the man who picked the wedding ring out of her hand.

For three days, courageous men tried to scale the tower walls. Some attempted to climb up, using long ladders and ropes, but the sides of the tower were too steep. Others tried to fly on homemade wings, but the wings fell apart before they got off the ground. The princess waited and waited, but no one even came close to reaching her.

Then, just as she was going to give up, one last contestant galloped into the square. He was shabbily dressed, but his horse was magnificent. It glowed like a rainbow.

As everyone stared, the rainbow horse unfolded huge wings.

The crowd gasped in amazement as the rainbow horse flew right up to where the princess was waiting. The young man on its back plucked the ring from the princess's hand, and – would you believe it – the princess smiled and blew him a kiss. The clever girl had found someone worthy of her at last. Not a baron or a count, but someone who knew how to use his brains. He was, as you might have guessed, our very own Miguel!

After the wedding, he returned the golden horseshoe to the rainbow horse with his thanks. The king of the flying horses had more than repaid him!

South America

The Rainbow Snake

A STORY FROM VENEZUELA

In the beginning, all the birds in the world had feathers that were plain grey, with not a coloured quill among them. They were quite happy to be grey. Then, one day, a cormorant came across a dead snake lying in the water at the edge of a lake. It was a rainbow snake, with lots of bright colours in its glossy scales.

The cormorant hopped into the water and dragged the snake ashore with his beak. "See what I have found," he said to a finch, who'd stopped to drink at the water's edge. "It must have just fallen out of the sky."

The finch hopped over to peer at the snake. "What wonderful colours," he sighed. "Even if I had just one of those colours in my feathers, it would make me look like a king."

"Look!" gasped the cormorant. "Some yellow from the snake has rubbed off onto your breast. You're right, you do look like a king now."

The finch stopped to admire his reflection in the water for a moment, then he flew into the sky, cheeping as he went, "Look at me! Look at me! I am grey no more!"

In less time than it takes for a morning flower to open, the shores of the lake were teeming with birds of every shape and size.

"Let me have some colours!"

"I want to be blue!"

"I want to be green!"

The ibis grabbed some scarlet. The kingbird fought with the flatbill and the toucan for the gold. The parrot snatched some green and orange. The nightjar helped himself to some brown, while the egret covered himself with dazzling white.

The finch spotted the cormorant standing to one side, still as grey as ever.

"Aren't you going to take some colours?" the finch asked him, confused. "After all, you were the one who found the rainbow snake."

"I will when everyone else has finished," said the cormorant. "I do not like all this squabbling."

The wise cormorant waited patiently until all the others had left, chattering excitedly and showing off their new colours. Then he inspected the rainbow snake. There weren't many colours left – in fact, just a few specks of white that the egret hadn't been able to reach.

"You have missed out," the finch said sadly. "Perhaps you should have picked your favourite colour before you told everyone else about the snake."

"I am quite happy to make do with white," said the cormorant. "After all, it's not the colours that make the bird, but his thoughts and actions."

The finch watched the cormorant flap away, and marvelled at his wisdom. He promised himself that he would try to live up to the cormorant's example. He was still delighted with his brand new yellow breast, though!

The forests of Venezuela are full of wonderfully coloured birds, but the noble cormorant is still grey, with just a few specks of white on his wings.

The Lost Friend

A STORY FROM COLOMBIA

No two men could have been more different, and yet they were best friends. Carrao was tall and thin, with a fiery temper. His fists were always ready for a scrap, he was afraid of nothing and no one. His friend Pedro was short and fat, with round glasses and a permanent smile on his face. He liked good food and good books. All he wanted was a peaceful life.

The two friends lived on ranches that were a few miles apart. They often had dinner at Pedro's house, because he was such a good cook.

One night, the two friends shared a wonderful dinner of fried beans with pork crackling, bananas, avocado and corncakes. After the meal, Pedro went to stand on his back porch. He looked up at the sky and frowned. Rolls of threatening dark-grey storm clouds were gathering on the horizon.

"It looks as if there's going to be a heavy storm. Why don't you spend the night here, Carrao?" he suggested.

"I am not afraid of storms," laughed Carrao, finishing his wine. "But I'd better get going before it starts raining. I don't want to get my new hat wet."

"If you're sure you'll be all right . . ." said Pedro. He knew it was useless to argue with his friend — Carrao was probably the most stubborn person in the whole world.

The thin man leapt over the gate to the corral, heading for his horse.

"See you tomorrow, friend."

"Safe journey, amigo," Pedro called after him.

Carrao hadn't been gone very long when the heavens opened. Rain lashed Pedro's house, flooding the corral and the porch. A gale blew across the savannah, uprooting trees and blowing buildings down. It was the worst storm Pedro had ever seen, and it raged all through the night.

"I hope Carrao got home safely," Pedro said to himself as he huddled under the blankets, listening to the wind whistling through his house. He turned over and after much tossing and turning, he went to sleep.

The next morning dawned bright and beautiful. Only the damage to buildings and trees showed that the storm had ever happened.

A cowboy knocked on Pedro's door.

"We have bad news, Señor . . ."

The cowboy held up Carrao's new hat, all squashed and covered in mud.

"He never got home . . ."

Pedro felt as if his heart was going to break in two. His best friend was lost! Perhaps he had fallen in some gulley or had got lost in some wood. If only he'd insisted that Carrao should stay the night, this might not have happened. His best friend would be safe . . .

Poor Pedro, who had never wanted adventure, just the comforts of home, made a vow. If Carrao was alive, he would find him and rescue him. Pedro was determined not to return home without him. So Pedro said goodbye to his neighbours, saddled his horse and rode out in search of his friend.

Pedro searched all over Colombia for the rest of his life, but he never did find Carrao. He never gave up, though. After his death, Pedro's spirit returned to earth in the shape of a brown marsh bird, a limpkin, so he could keep searching. The limpkin is also known as the crying bird, because of its loud, wailing call. If you ever go to Colombia, you might hear it flying around, calling out for its long-lost friend, "Carr-aao! Carraa-ooooo!"

Two for You, Three for Me

A STORY FROM ECUADOR

An old man and his wife had five eggs to share between them. "I'll have three and you can have the other two," said the old man, Juan.

"I'll have three, thank you," said his wife, Juana. "After all, I boiled them."

"But I fetched them from the market," argued the old man.

Juana slapped his hand away. "If I don't have three, I'll die, and nothing, but nothing, will make me come back from the dead to do your cooking and your cleaning."

"Go ahead and die," laughed Juan. "You're only having two."

Juana lay down on the bed. She closed her eyes and crossed her hands on her chest like a corpse.

"Don't be silly, Juana," said the old man. "Your eggs are getting cold."

His wife did not reply.

"If you don't get up so we can have supper, I'm going to call Father Martin," said Juan.

He went and fetched the priest, who anointed Juana's forehead with holy oils.

"You're making a fool of yourself," Juan whispered in Juana's ear. "Come and have two eggs."

"I want three or nothing," Juana hissed back.

"If you don't come and eat," threatened Juan, "I'm going to call the mourners. Then the whole neighbourhood will hear of your folly."

Juana opened just one eye. "Call them. I'm not going to give in."

So all the women in the village gathered around Juana's bed and started wailing and crying. They smashed all Juana's pots, as was the custom of the village.

"Your best crockery is gone," Juan whispered in Juana's ear. "Now stop being silly and have your supper. Two eggs are enough for you."

"Over my dead body," came back the reply.

"So be it," said Juan. He fetched the undertaker, who put Juana in a coffin.

"This has gone too far, my love," Juan muttered to Juana, pretending to kiss his apparently dead wife on the lips. "I beg you, sit up and eat."

"Two eggs or three?"

"Two."

"I might as well be dead, then."

"You stubborn woman!" hissed Juan angrily. "It seems you really are ready to meet your maker."

He nodded to the undertaker's men, who nailed the lid on the coffin and carried it to the graveyard. The priest said a final blessing.

"Please, lower it carefully," sobbed Juan. He was the first to scatter a handful of soil on the coffin. That's when Juana screeched and started knocking on the lid. She had no intention of being buried alive.

"All right, you win, Juan!" she screamed. "I'll have two eggs."

The pair of them raced home, leaving the rest of the villagers standing around, scratching their heads. Juana got there first. She stuffed one egg in her mouth, then a second — and then a third.

"I win after all," she cried.

Silly Juana! Silly Juan!

Wish Upon a Star

A STORY FROM PERU

A young shepherd named Felipe sat under a kapok tree, lost in thought. He was getting married in a couple of months, but how was he going to provide everything that he and his bride needed, like a new home? How was he going to feed his children when they came? If only he had some money — then he could buy a couple of llamas and start a herd! But as it was, his prospects looked bleak.

An old man interrupted his reverie. "May I sit with you for a while? It's cold tonight."

Felipe made space on his rug. He offered the stranger the last hunk of bread in his satchel, the last drop of milk in his flask.

"You are very kind," said the old man, "so I am going to tell you a secret. Look up at the sky — what do you see?"

Felipe turned his face to the heavens. "I see thousands of stars. There's the Milky Way."

"Look closer," instructed the old man. "Can you see any other stars?"

"Yes," said Felipe. "I can see a constellation called the Yacana, the Llama."

"Every night the Yacana takes a stroll along the Milky Way," explained the old man. "Some nights we see it, some nights we don't. Often it stops to have a drink from the Milky Way. If it ever stops right above you, make a wish. Legend has it that standing below the Yacana constellation brings good luck."

"Is that really true?" asked the young man.

The stranger shrugged, stood up and fastened his cloak around him. "You won't know until you've tried. Goodnight, and good luck, amigo."

When the stranger had gone, Felipe looked up at the sky again. How bright the stars looked, and how close they seemed! He felt he could stand on tiptoe and pluck them like cherries from a tree.

And there was the Yacana, moving slowly, majestically, along the Milky Way. He could see its eyes clearly – he could even make out the shape of its neck.

The Yacana stopped. Was it drinking from the Milky Way as the old man had said? Was there any truth in the old legend?

Felipe closed his eyes and wished very hard. *Please, let me earn enough money to buy a house, to support my future wife and children.*

As he wished, something brushed past his face. He opened his eyes to see tiny clouds fluttering down from the stars, carried by the breeze. He reached out to catch one. It was a bundle of newly shorn wool – llama wool. How soft and warm it felt in his hands!

"The Yacana must have sent it," said the young peasant. "Thank you, Yacana. Thank you!"

He ran around the field, picking the wool off the ground, untangling it from the branches of the kapok tree. Above him, the Yacana continued to move across the sky. The horizon was turning pink and the stars were starting to fade. Felipe realized that it was nearly dawn.

Later that day, he took the wool to a merchant in town, hoping to get a good price for it.

"I have never seen such fine llama wool before!" said the merchant. "And look at the colours: the pink of dawn, the blue of a clear day, the red of sunset, the velvet black of a summer night, the silvery white of shining stars . . . why, all the colours of the sky seemed to be caught in this wool!"

He paid the shepherd a good sum, enough to buy two llamas, so he could start a herd. Felipe hurried to give his bride the good news. Life was going to be good for them, thanks to the llama in the sky!

The Armadillo's Song

A STORY FROM BOLIVIA

The armadillo was old – too old to dig, to swim, to do anything but snuffle in the earth for ants. *If I could sing*, he thought, *it would take my mind off the pain of being old and alone.*

He heard a cricket singing in a carob tree. "Teach me to sing," he begged. "I wish I could while away the time making music like you."

"We do not sing to while away the time," said the cricket. "We sing because we are in love. Find someone to love and you too will sing beautifully."

"Alas," said the old armadillo, "I am too old to find someone to love."

The frogs started singing and he creaked over to their pond.

"Teach me to sing like you," he asked one of them.

"We sing to call our mates home," said the frog. "Have you a loved one to call home?"

"No," said the armadillo sadly. "I have no one to call my own."

The moon sank below the horizon and the sun peeped over the hills at the edge of the grassland. The armadillo pricked up his ears. Someone else was singing, performing a song – a song even more beautiful than the chirruping of the crickets or the croaking of the frogs!

The armadillo was entranced. "Who is singing?" he cried. "Show yourself!"

There was a rustle and a bird appeared, hopping along a branch. It was a young tapaculo.

"I would give anything to sing like you," said the armadillo.

"I have just escaped from a cage. Now I sing because I am free," replied the bird. "Are you not free to sing?"

"No," said the armadillo. "I am an old creature trapped in an old shell. Time has made me a prisoner."

"Go and see the wise wizard who lives by the river," said the tapaculo. "He helped me to get my freedom. Perhaps he will give you the gift of song."

The wizard was collecting dew from the leaves of a plant when the armadillo arrived. He listened to his problem, then said, "You do not need my help. Wait until you too are free, and then you will sing even better than the tapaculo in the tree."

The armadillo did not understand. Only death could free him from his heavy shell, his tired feet, his aching claws. How would he be able to sing then? He sat down to think about it and soon fell asleep — never to wake again!

A few months later, a young farmer found an old armadillo shell under a bush. He cleaned it and polished it, then stretched guitar strings across the hollow side. He made a charango, a guitar.

His bride came out listen to him play. What a beautiful sound the charango made! It was sweeter than a cricket or a frog — sweeter even than a tapaculo in the wild.

The wizard's promise to the armadillo had come true after all.

Toad in the Hole

A STORY FROM PARAGUAY

There was to be a great concert in the sky, organized by the full moon itself. All the birds were invited.

"Are you going?" Toad asked Vulture.

"But of course," replied Vulture rather vainly. "No musical soirée is complete without my guitar music."

"I wish I had wings," said Toad. "Then the very heavens would echo with the sound of my singing."

On the night of the concert, Vulture flew up into the sky with his guitar tucked under his right wing. Just wait until the others heard him play. They would not be able to resist dancing to his music!

"Good evening, everyone," he said to the other birds.

There was a titter among the guests as something crawled out of his guitar.

"Why, Mr Toad," exclaimed Flamingo. "How nice of you to join us."

"I do apologize for stowing away in your guitar," Toad said to Vulture. "It was the only way I could get here."

Vulture was furious. He'd been tricked into dragging a slimy creature into the skies, the home of the birds and stars. But he would get his revenge . . .

At the end of the concert, he smiled at Toad. "I assume you wish to return home the way you came, sir?"

"If you don't mind a passenger in your guitar again," beamed Toad.

Vulture bowed his head. "I would never desert a fellow musician in his hour of need. Hop in."

Toad hopped into Vulture's guitar and clung onto the strings.

"Here we go!" called Vulture.

He took off, soaring into the blossoming dawn. He flew over the prairie and the forests, and when he reached a rocky outcrop bristling with jagged spikes, he tipped the guitar over.

Down Toad fell, turning head over heels until he hit the ground far below. He broke his back in a dozen different places and it stayed all lumpy when it healed. Poor Toad's voice was never the same again. Fear had turned his beautiful singing voice into a horrible croak!

The Three Oranges

A STORY FROM BRAZIL

A young Brazilian named Luis Fernando came across an old woman carrying a bundle of sticks. "Let me help you," he said, taking them from her.

"Where are you headed, young one?"

"I am off to travel my country. I want to see the Amazon, the rain forest, the beaches . . . "

"Our country is a fine place to see indeed," the old woman agreed. When they reached her home, she fished three oranges out of her pocket. "These will keep you going for a while," she said, "but cut them open only when you are close to water."

Luis Fernando continued his journey and before long he was lost in a desert. When he could bear the thirst no longer, he cut open one of the oranges, even though there was no water nearby. A young woman with golden hair tumbled out. "Water, water!" she gasped, clutching her throat,

and in a puff of desert sand, she was gone.

Luis Fernando continued walking. The sun beat down mercilessly on his head till he could think of nothing but orange juice to cool his parched throat. He split the second orange open and, once more, a girl with golden hair tumbled out, cried, "Water, water!" and disappeared in a puff of dry dust.

By now Luis Fernando was nearly dead with thirst. But he didn't dare cut the third orange open till he had found his way into the forest and was standing by a stream. This time, when he cut into the orange and the girl with golden hair cried, "Water, water!" he was able to give her some. He fell in love with her immediately and asked her to marry him. The girl, equally smitten, accepted straightaway.

"But I must get you some nice clothes before I introduce you to my family," said Luis Fernando. "Those rags won't do. Wait here for me."

The girl hid in a tree to wait. While she was sitting there, a hideous witch with only one eye came to fill her jar in the stream. She saw the girl peeking through the leaves and said, "How beautiful you are, my dear. You would make a beautiful bride."

"I am going to get married soon," said the girl.

The witch's face creased into a smile. "Is that so? Then come and I shall comb your golden hair for you. A man likes his bride to have neat hair."

The girl came down shyly and put her head on the witch's lap. The slow movement of the comb through her hair made her feel drowsy and, when she was nearly asleep, the witch took a pin from her pocket and stuck it in the girl's hand. Instantly, the girl changed into a bird and flew away with the pin still stuck in her wing.

Not long afterwards, the young man returned for his bride.

"The sun has burnt my skin and I don't want you to see me like this," said the witch, who had taken the girl's place in the tree. "Give me a veil to hide my face."

Luis Fernando passed her his scarf to use as a veil. The witch clambered down and, holding the scarf across her face, went to Luis Fernando's house in place of the beautiful girl. No matter how much the young man begged, she would not let him see her ugly, one-eyed face. "You must be patient and wait till my sunburn heals," she told him.

By the day of the wedding, Luis Fernando still had not been able to look at his bride's face again. "Will she let me lift her veil, to kiss her at the wedding?" he wondered, sitting at his window. "I would like to very much, sunburn or not."

A bird settled on the branch of a tree outside his window and started to sing a sad, sad song.

How sad, thought Luis Fernando, *and on my wedding day too*. He reached out and caressed the bird's head. "How tame you are. Why are you so troubled, little bird?"

The bird hopped onto his lap, looking up at him trustingly. Luis Fernando noticed that there was something stuck in its wing. *Probably a thorn*, he thought, and pulled it out. When he looked at it, he realized it was a pin, not a thorn. "Who would do this to a bird?" he cried.

In an instant, the bird turned back into his bride. "A cruel witch enchanted me," she said, "and now she's pretending to be me!"

Luis Fernando called guards to seize the one-eyed witch. The girl put on her wedding dress and married her loving Luis Fernando. The two of them lived out their days in the Brazilian sun, as happy as happy can be.

The Man in the Moon

A STORY FROM ARGENTINA

Once upon a time there was a beautiful girl called Amata who lived in a little village surrounded by forests at the foot of a high mountain. Amata was a dreamer, full of strange ideas. She imagined that there was a man in the moon who smiled down at her every night.

"I want to marry him, Mama," she said stubbornly. "He is the most handsome man I have ever seen."

"There is no man in the moon," her mother snapped. "It is time you put away your childish dreams. A lot of men in the village have asked for your hand in marriage. You must forget about the moon and choose one of them."

But Amata wanted no one if she couldn't have the man in the moon. That night, she put her few belongings in a bag and crept out of the village. She would visit the man of her dreams and tell him how much she loved him. Surely he would answer her?

Amata wandered through the forest, peering up through the trees. The moon lived so high up in the night sky – how could she reach him? She tried calling out to him, but her voice was drowned out by the sound of night creatures. She climbed the tallest tree in the forest, trying to reach out to him, tearing her dress on the sharp twigs. Still the moon was too far away.

Amata clambered down from the tree and sat down to think. At last it occurred to her to climb up the mountain. Surely she could reach the moon from the summit?

Up the mountain path she went, following the ancient tracks made by the shepherds, leaving the warm forest far behind. The snow on the mountain turned her bare feet blue, and sharp stones cut her little feet, but she took no notice. She was getting nearer to the man she loved; nothing else mattered.

At the very summit of the mountain, she stood on tiptoe and called, "Hello . . . hello . . ."

Still the man in the moon was out of reach. Rain clouds drew a curtain around him and he disappeared from view. The poor girl struggled back down the mountain, sobbing in despair. She was determined not to go back to her village. If she couldn't have the man in the moon, she would marry no one.

In the forest, she stopped to bathe her tired feet in a lake. And would you believe it, there was the moon, free of the clouds, floating on the water. Amata had gone to the top of a mountain to reach him, but there he was, right at her feet. How handsome he looked, and how pleased to see her. She reached out to caress his face — and fell headlong into the lake. The last thing she saw was his smile . . .

High among the stars, the god Tupa could not bear to see such pain. Such a brave girl deserved a better fate, a happier ending. The god blinked and Amata floated back to the surface of the water, transformed into a magnificent water lily.

Even today, the lily and the man in the moon still meet on the lake every night to gaze at each other's undying beauty.

The Monk's Treasure

A STORY FROM CHILE

A cattleman was walking past an old barn when he spied a sack leaning against the door. "Help!" came a voice from inside it. "In God's name, assist me!"

The cattleman untied the sack hurriedly.

"God sent you to release me, my son," said the voice, and out of the sack stepped a monk in a tattered habit.

"What happened, Father? What were you doing in there?" the cattleman asked.

"I was put in there by four wicked thieves," replied the monk. "Would you believe it, they wanted to give me all their stolen gold! They couldn't keep it after I heard their confession. Of course, I had to say no. I explained that monks couldn't own anything. Those awful thieves threatened to drown me in the river if I didn't take it. They tied me up in the sack, ready to throw me into the water."

"And where are the thieves now, Father?" asked the cattleman.

"They're in the house, having dinner. As soon as they finish, they'll come out for me."

"I don't mind taking stolen gold, Father," said the cattleman, who was starting to think this might work out well for him. "If you will tie me up in that sack, I'll pretend to be you. I'll tell the thieves I changed my mind. It's so dark tonight, they'll never know I'm not really you."

The monk clapped his hands. "It's as if God is rewarding you for helping me. Of course I will." He exchanged his habit for the cattleman's clothes and tied him up in the sack. The cattleman waited there in the stuffy sack for the thieves to come. When he heard their footsteps, he shouted, "I'll take your loot! I'll take every single golden coin you have."

To his horror, the thieves took no notice of what he was saying. Instead, they bundled him onto a cart, took him down to the river and threw him in. He struggled to free himself, but the

bag was tied too tightly. He had just given himself up for dead when someone dragged the bag onto the riverbank and ripped the bag open. It was the monk!

"Father, you've saved me!" the cattleman gasped.

"You'd better not call me 'Father'," the monk said with a chuckle. "I am not really a monk."

"Who are you, then?" the cattleman asked, confused.

"My name is Pedro de Urdemalas," the fake monk said, and bowed with a flourish.

The cattleman had heard of Pedro de Urdemalas before. Everyone in Chile had. Pedro was a scoundrel, a famous trickster.

"I dressed up as a monk to beg for money from people," said Pedro. "When I came across the thieves and spotted their gold, I tried to steal it. As a punishment, they decided to throw me in the river, which is when you came along."

"I nearly drowned!" spluttered the cattleman.

"Give me back my habit," said Pedro, "and I really will make you rich. But I need to borrow your cattle too."

Shortly afterwards, the thieves were woken up by a strange sound. A monk was singing a hymn outside their house. They recognized his voice at once.

"It's the monk we drowned in the river!" gasped one of the thieves. "His ghost has come back to haunt us."

"Good fortune has befallen me, brothers," called out Pedro. "Come and see what providence has thrown my way."

The thieves peeped cautiously out of a window. "Are you a ghost?"

"I am alive and well," replied Pedro. "Fairies rescued me. They have a whole city at the bottom of the river, with houses and fields and schools for the little ones. They gave me these fine cattle, look. I am set up for life."

The thieves eyed the cows with envy. If only they had a herd like that, they would have no need to go around robbing people. They could settle down and live honestly.

"I'm sure you could have your own herd if you visited the fairies," said Pedro. "The king of the fairies gives gifts like this to all his guests."

"Why don't you put us in sacks?" suggested the thieves. "Throw us in the river, please."

"With pleasure!" laughed Pedro.

An hour or so later, Pedro and the cattleman tipped four heavy sacks into a boat that was moored on the river. Pedro cut the moorings and the little boat slid away downstream.

"With luck, the river will take the boat all the way to Santiago," he said.

"Which gives us plenty of time to make off with their gold," added the cattleman.

Pedro chuckled. "And plenty of time to spend it!"

Europe

Cap O' Rushes

A baron had three daughters: a tall, greedy one, a fat, competitive one, and a young, thoughtful one. One evening, he asked them, "How much do you love me?"

"As much as kings love gold," said the tall one. The baron was delighted with her answer, and gave her a purse full of golden trinkets.

"As much as queens love diamonds," said the fat one. The baron kissed her and gave her a sparkling tiara to show how pleased he was.

"I love you as much as food loves salt," said the youngest.

The baron frowned. Salt cost nothing. Was his youngest daughter saying her love for him was worthless?

"Our dear sister insults you," whispered the tall, greedy one.

"She doesn't love you at all," murmured the fat, competitive one.

The baron had heard enough. He threw his youngest daughter out of the house without money or clothes or anything to eat. She had nothing but the beautiful dress she was wearing. The poor girl walked away from her father's house, weeping as she went. After a long time, she came to some marshes. She picked a bundle of rushes and plaited them into a dress with a hood, then hid her pretty dress inside a hollow tree.

Close to the marsh, there was a grand house. The girl knocked on the door, and a haughty butler answered it.

"Please sir, I am seeking employment," she said.

"Go round to the back door," the butler sneered. "The front door is for guests, not servants."

The girl went to the back door, where the cook took her on to wash the pans and scrub the floor. She wouldn't give her name, so because of her hooded dress, they called her Cap o' Rushes.

A young prince lived nearby. His parents were organizing a grand ball so he could find a wife. It would be held over three nights and all the young women of the land were invited.

"We are going to watch the guests arrive," said the other servants. "Will you come with us?"

"I'm too busy cleaning the pans," she replied. But when they had left, she fetched her beautiful frock from the tree and went to the ball, where the prince asked her to dance. They made a beautiful couple, twirling round the ballroom.

At midnight, Cap o' Rushes hurried back to hide her dress. When the servants returned, they said, "There was a mysterious girl there who stole the prince's heart. Come with us tomorrow and see."

"I'll be too busy scrubbing the floor," said Cap o' Rushes. But the next day, when the servants had left, she fetched her gown and went to the ball again.

"Dance with me," begged the prince. And the pair danced all night, without stopping for a drink or a bite to eat.

At midnight Cap o' Rushes hurried away again. When her friends returned, they said, "That beautiful stranger was there again. Come to the ball and see."

"I shall be too busy darning my socks," said Cap o' Rushes. But of course she put on her beautiful dress once more and went to the ball.

This time, the prince was waiting for her with a little box. Inside was a gold ring. "Marry me," said the prince, going down on one knee.

Cap o' Rushes accepted, and there was much joy in the palace. Wedding invitations were sent out to all the important people in the land, including Cap o' Rushes' father. Everyone was very excited at the thought of going to a grand wedding feast. Well, almost everyone. Cap o' Rushes' father missed his beautiful, thoughtful daughter. He bitterly regretted sending her away. How she would have loved the wedding!

On the day before she was to be married, Cap o' Rushes went to see the cook who was preparing the wedding feast. "Do not put salt in the food," she instructed her. "Nor are you to place salt cellars on the dining tables."

"That will make the food taste fair horrible, my lady," protested the cook.

"I know," said Cap o' Rushes, "but, please, humour me."

At the wedding feast, the food was piled high on the tables. Everyone nibbled at this and that, but no one ate more than a spoonful. The food, with not a grain of salt in it, was absolutely tasteless.

Cap o' Rushes' father, who was sitting sadly on his own, burst into tears.

"What's the matter, sir?" asked Cap o' Rushes from behind her lacy veil.

"I had a daughter who swore she loved me as much as food loves salt. Now I realize she loved me more than anyone in the world."

"And what happened to your daughter, sir?" asked the groom.

"I threw her out," bawled Cap o' Rushes' father. "She must have drowned in the marshes or been murdered by thieves."

"No," said Cap o' Rushes, standing up. "Your daughter is alive and loves you still." And she removed her veil so her father could see her face.

So father and daughter were reunited, and remembered how much they loved each other every time they sprinkled salt on their food.

The Selkie Wife

A STORY FROM SCOTLAND

A young fisherman spied five girls playing in the surf, their cloaks strewn on the rocks around them. He realized that they were selkies, magical creatures that could change from seals to human beings and back again. Silently, the fisherman reached out from behind a rock and –

"Watch out, sisters!"

The five selkies jumped up like salmon leaping a weir. Four of them grabbed their cloaks and disappeared into the water. But the youngest was left behind. The fisherman held her sealskin, a wicked grin on his face.

"Please, sir. Give it back. I'll pay you for it with pearls from the bottom of the sea."

"You don't want to go back to the sea, missy. Stay and be my wife. I'm considered quite a catch in this part of the world."

The selkie could tell from the fisherman's eyes that he had fallen in love with her. She could also detect a hint of stubbornness in his character that told her she was not going to get her sealskin back. And without it, she was trapped on land, unable to turn herself into a seal again.

"Very well then. If trapped I must be, let me be trapped by love," she said.

To the fisherman's great delight, the beautiful selkie seemed to like her new life on land. They had a grand wedding with music; they built a little cottage on the brow of a hill and, in time, they had seven children – four boys and three girls, all as beautiful and handsome as the morning sun in autumn. After the first year of marriage, the selkie never mentioned the sea again.

The children grew up – the boys to be fishermen like their father, the girls to help their mother on the farm. One day, the youngest daughter returned home with a cut foot.

"Fetch me a piece of cloth," said the selkie, "and I'll bind it up for you."

The girl searched for a clean rag and came back with a large piece of dark material in her arms. The selkie's heart missed a beat the moment she saw it. "Where did you find that?"

"It was hidden in the mattress. I saw Pa taking it out one day. He kissed it, Ma, and then he stuffed it back in. May we cut a strip from it?"

Inside the mattress! So that's where the sealskin had been hidden all these years. To think the selkie had never guessed it was right under her nose.

"Give it here, girl." The selkie's trembling hand closed over the sealskin and instantly her mind was flooded with old memories: her home at the bottom of the sea, her sisters playing in the waves, her father calling them in for dinner. If only she could see her people just one more time . . .

"Get the dinner ready, child," the selkie said, quickly binding the girl's foot with her apron. "I must go out, but I shall be back soon."

The fisherman, rowing home with his four sons, saw a seal diving joyously through the waves and his heart turned over. He knew right away it was his wife.

"Do not fear, fisherman. I'll come home again . . ."

But the selkie never did return. Who knows what kept her at the bottom of the ocean? The poor fisherman often roamed the shore at night, calling out for his love, but the only reply was the sound of the waves beating against the rocks.

The Island of Fairies

A STORY FROM WALES

The old graveyard stood on top of a cliff, lonely and neglected, its gravestones leaning in the wind. Gruffyd pushed open the creaking gate. He liked coming here to look out across the sea, to sit quietly and think about his wife, who was buried in the churchyard. But today there was something strange about the view. Gruffyd stopped and frowned. There, on the surface of the sea, was an island. Gruffyd could make out hills and valleys and a harbour with a lighthouse.

Strange that I never noticed that island before, thought Gruffyd. *I shall pay it a visit.*

He hurried down to the harbour where his little fishing boat was moored. But where was the mysterious island? Standing at the prow of his boat, he couldn't see it at all. Had his eyes been playing a trick on him? Had he imagined it? He ran back to the graveyard to check. No, there it was. Light was beaming from the lighthouse. Smoke rose from little household chimneys.

Gruffyd stepped forward to get a better view — and the island disappeared again. He took a step backwards and the island reappeared. "I can only see the island from this particular spot," said Gruffyd, "but I'm determined to visit it."

Using his penknife, he gently lifted the piece of turf at his feet and took it down to his boat. Standing on it, he looked out to sea. Now he could make out the island, its hills bathed in the

light of the rising moon, its lighthouse winking as he neared the shore.

"Ahoy there!"

Welcoming people crowded onto the jetty, hands reaching out to moor his boat. What beautiful folk they were, their hair as red as autumn fire, their eyes as green as the water in deep wells. Suddenly, Gruffyd realized they were fairies. They had wings growing out of their backs; their feet hardly touched the ground as they moved about. He was on a fairy island!

The young ones were very excited to meet him. They'd never seen a human being before, or spoken to one.

"How did you find us?" asked the king of the island. "Our island is invisible to human eyes."

"I stood on a particular patch of grass," explained Gruffyd, "up in St David's graveyard."

The fabled patch of turf! All the fairies had heard about it in stories and lullabies. Legend had it that it marked the spot where a fairy queen had shed tears for her mortal husband, who had died from old age. Many fairies had searched for it, but none had found it. They worried that humans would try to steal their fairy treasure if they knew about the island.

The fairies gave Gruffyd fairy cakes to eat and fairy wine to drink. The young danced for him, whirling so fast in the night that they looked like fireflies. All too soon, the cock crowed and morning light spread across the sky. The fairies led Gruffyd back to his boat. The king held out a bag of gold.

"In return for the turf," he said.

Gruffyd knew that if he gave the king the piece of turf, he would never find the island again. Even so, he could not turn down such a generous offer. The gold would set him up for the rest of his life, so he took it. At any rate, he would always know that the fairies were there, floating on the water, even if he couldn't see them!

The Giant's Causeway

Benandonner, the Scottish giant, peered across the sea to the Irish coast. "Hey, Finn McCool, you little weakling," he shouted. "Are you picking weeds to eat for your dinner?"

Finn had been pulling up potatoes. He straightened up and grunted with anger. His Scottish rival was said to be twice his size, but he, Finn of the Fianna, was a respected warrior. He was not going to take insults from anyone.

"Why don't you go and wash your filthy mouth out, Benandonner? I can smell your breath from over here," he shouted.

The Scot bared teeth as big as tombstones. "Are you calling me unwashed?"

"As dirty as a horsefly in dung."

Benandonner's scowl was visible from across the sea. "Thank your lucky stars I can't swim, Finn McCool, or I'd come and crush you."

"Crush me, you big oaf?" Finn boomed in reply. "You couldn't swat a fly if it landed on your warty nose. Stop making excuses. I'll build you a bridge, Benandonner, so you can meet me face to face."

He tore a lump of rock from the cliff and hurled it into the water. It landed with a splash that flooded half the fields in County Antrim.

"Here's a stepping stone for you, Benandonner."
SPLASH!

"And here's another." SPLASH!

"And another." SPLASH!

"Finn," said his wife, Oonah, "what are you doing?"

"Let the oaf try and crush me," Finn snapped. "I've always wanted to tackle that silly lump of gristle."

He continued throwing enormous boulders into the sea until he'd built a bridge, a causeway, right across the channel from Mull to Ireland. "There you are, Benandonner. You can come and get me whenever you like."

The bridge started to shake as the Scot tested the first boulder with his enormous feet.

"Finn, you're in no fit state to fight!" Oonah exclaimed. "You must be exhausted from throwing boulders."

"Let him come," bragged Finn. "I'll flatten him."

"Nonsense," said Oonah. "You couldn't flatten a sheet of paper if you sat on it. Go and lie in the field behind the house. I'll think of something."

It was getting dark when the Scottish giant stepped heavily on to the Irish shore. He really was much bigger than Finn McCool.

Oonah was standing there, ankle-deep in the water, waiting for him.

"Are you Finn's wife?" he asked.

"Yes, but Finn's not here," replied Oonah, her hands firmly on her hips. "He went to get milk for the babby."

"Finn's got children?"

Oonah nodded. "A son. I've just put him to bed out in the field, so don't go waking him up."

"You let the baby sleep outside?"

"Only three months old and he's too big to fit in the house already," Oonah beamed proudly. "He'll be as big as his father when he's fully grown. Come and see."

Finn's baby lay wrapped in a blanket that stretched from one end of the potato field to the other. He was sucking an enormous thumb.

"Only three months old," gasped Benandonner, trying to keep the awe out of his voice. Finn

had always seemed smaller than Benandonner from across the channel, but if the baby was this huge, there was no telling how enormous his father would be. Benandonner was beginning to wonder if he might have made a terrible mistake.

"I can't wait to get my hands on your insolent husband," he said to Oonah, keeping his voice low so he wouldn't wake the baby, "but I forgot to take the porridge off the fire, I was in such a rush to get here. Mustn't let it burn."

"No sense in letting good porridge go to waste," agreed Oonah. "Now that Finn has built a causeway, you can come and thrash him anytime."

"You can tell your husband I'll be back tomorrow," said Benandonner. "I don't take insults from anyone."

"I'll pass the message on."

The Scottish giant scurried down to the shore, and Oonah could hear him tearing the boulders out of the causeway as he raced home. He wanted to make absolutely sure that Finn wouldn't follow him.

She poked the baby with her toe. "Finn, take your filthy thumb out of your mouth. You can stop pretending now. Benandonner's gone."

Finn sat up, pulling the blanket away from his face.

"Good idea of ours to trick Benandonner into thinking I was my own son," he grinned.

"Yes, aren't *we* clever," Oonah snapped, heading in to roast a cow for dinner. "Brains will always beat brawn in the end."

A Proper Princess

A STORY FROM DENMARK

The crown prince of Denmark, Prince Johan, decided he was old enough and clever enough to get married. All that he needed was a proper princess to be his bride. But where could he find a real princess in this world of commoners? He met all of the princesses in Denmark, but none of them was quite royal enough for him, however lovely they looked or beautifully they spoke.

His father lent him the royal carriage, his mother had the royal luggage brought out and dusted, and off he went around the world, looking for a bride. After many months, he returned empty-handed to Copenhagen. He'd met so many beautiful, well-dressed, well-mannered girls, but none had turned out to be a real princess who he could share his kingdom with.

"I'll never marry. Perhaps I should become a monk," he sighed sadly.

A few nights later, there was a terrible, sky-splitting storm. It rained. It thundered. The wind howled around the palace. The prince heard a tap on the door and he opened it, to find a girl standing on the doorstep, soaked to the skin.

"May I come and shelter here? My name is Princess Anna," she said.

Not another girl pretending to be a princess! Prince Johan shook his head as his mother welcomed the girl. No princess would wander about in a storm. Her dress was muddy, water seeped out of her satin shoes, and there was a frog in her pocket. And yet she kept insisting she was royal — as royal as he was himself!

"I know I don't look like a princess, but I am. I got lost on my way to finishing school," Princess Anna said sweetly.

Finishing school! As if a true princess would need to go to finishing school. The prince sighed to himself. Another unsuitable girl, even if she was far prettier than any of the others.

"She might be telling the truth," whispered his mother, pouring some tea. "I'll try to find out."

66

While Princess Anna nibbled home-made ginger biscuits, the queen crept upstairs to the guest bedroom. She clapped her hands and servants came running.

"Put this dried pea under the mattress, right in the middle of the bed. Now fetch more mattresses, nineteen of them. Put them on top of each other. We shall see if Anna is a real princess."

By the time the servants were finished, the twenty mattresses almost reached the ceiling. "What kind people," said Princess Anna to herself, clambering up the side of the bed. "Home-made ginger biscuits, fresh tea and a cosy sky-high bed."

She rested her head on the soft pillows, thinking how charming and handsome Prince Johan was. She would dream of his blue eyes and chestnut-brown hair tonight. She snuggled under the warm blankets. But *ouch!* What was that?

In the morning, she came downstairs yawning and rubbing her eyes. "There was something hard under the mattresses," she said. "I didn't sleep a wink."

The queen turned to Prince Johan triumphantly. Only a real princess would be delicate enough to feel a pea through twenty thick mattresses. Prince Johan understood right away. He went down on one knee and asked Princess Anna to marry him.

She said yes — she had liked him from the moment he had opened the door — and their wedding was the best royal wedding there had ever been, with pea soup for starters and fresh peas with the roast beef.

Three Billy Goats Gruff

A STORY FROM NORWAY

Big Billy Goat Gruff, Medium Billy Goat Gruff, and snow-white Little Billy Goat Gruff lived together in a meadow beside a beautiful brook. Big Billy Goat Gruff was the eldest, and his brothers looked up to him. Whatever he did, they did too.

When summer came, the grass in the meadow went brown and the brook dried up. The goats decided to go to the hills, where there were often rain showers. There the grass was still green and water gurgled in the streams. Off they went, clip-clopping along the cobbled roads, Little Billy Goat Gruff leading the way, Medium Billy Goat Gruff hurrying along behind him, and Big Billy Goat Gruff bringing up the rear. Soon they came to a little wooden bridge. Under it lived a hideous, flesh-munching, bone-crunching troll.

"Who goes there?" roared the troll when he heard Little Billy Goat Gruff's tiny hooves rattling across the bridge.

"It's only me," said Little Billy Goat Gruff. "I'm going to the hills to get fat on green grass and fresh water."

"It is I who will get fat on you," growled the troll. "I'm coming to gobble you up."

"Oh please don't eat me," bleated Little Billy Goat Gruff, trembling in terror. "I'm only skin and bones. Wait till my brother comes along. He's much bigger than me."

"All right, be off with you, then," snarled the troll.

Before too long, the troll heard the sound of hooves again. Medium Billy Goat Gruff was overhead, clip-clopping along the bridge.

"Who goes there?" the troll bellowed from under the planks.

"It's me," said Medium Billy Goat Gruff. "I'm going to the hills to get fat on green grass and fresh water."

"It is I who will get fat on you," snickered the troll. "I'm coming to gobble you up."

"Please don't eat me," pleaded the second Billy Goat Gruff, his teeth chattering with fear. "I'm not much more than a bundle of goat hair. Wait till my big brother comes along. He's much, much bigger than me."

"All right, then," sniffed the troll, "be off with you."

By and by, the troll heard Big Billy Goat Gruff stamping across the bridge. He was so heavy that the planks creaked under his weight.

"Who goes there?" shouted the troll. He was getting very, very hungry.

"It is I, Big Billy Goat Gruff," answered the goat. "I am going to the hills to get fat on green grass and fresh water."

"It is I who will get fat on you," sneered the troll. "I'm coming to gobble you up."

Big Billy Goat Gruff laughed back and said, "Come and try. I'm not afraid of you."

The troll jumped out from under the bridge, but Big Billy Goat Gruff wasn't frightened of him at all. He leapt forward, butting the troll with his long, curved horns. He crushed him to bits. The dead troll fell in the river and was washed away, never to be seen again.

Little Billy Goat Gruff and Medium Billy Goat Gruff capered for joy as Big Billy Goat Gruff came to join them on the other side of the bridge. They headed for the hills, and all summer long they feasted on green grass and fresh water.

Nail Soup

Old Hanna's tummy was rumbling. What should she cook? Beef stew with dumplings, perhaps, or fried eggs with pickles and thick gravy.

A sound came from outside. She waddled over to the window to look. A tramp was poking around in the bushes.

"Can I help you?" Hanna asked crossly.

"I'm looking for berries, ma'am. Sorry to disturb you."

Hanna felt a little bit sorry for the tramp. But then, why didn't he get a job, earn some money? Then he'd have enough for food and drink.

"I'd invite you in, but I have no food in the house."

"That's all right, ma'am," said the tramp. "I don't need food. The berries are for my pudding."

Hanna couldn't help laughing. "You have a pudding, do you? And what's your main course?"

"I have all the ingredients in my pocket," answered the tramp. He rummaged around in his filthy jacket and pulled out a huge nail. "It makes the best nail soup in the world."

Hanna had never heard such nonsense. Was the tramp poking fun at her?

"If I could borrow a saucepan and some water, I'd show you how to make it," said the tramp.

The old woman fetched water in a pan. *Humour him*, she thought. *Nail soup, indeed. A likely story.*

The tramp dropped the nail into the saucepan and placed it on the fire he had made.

"Used it five times already," said the tramp. "Nourishing, filling soup every time. Of course, if I had just a dash of salt and pepper, it would be even more delicious."

Salt and pepper cost next to nothing. Hanna thought she might as well let the old tramp have them.

"It'll boil in a minute," said the tramp, sprinkling the salt and pepper into the soup. "Sadly,

this is not going to be the most delicious nail soup I've ever made. I've used the same nail five times, so the flavour is running a bit thin. Now if I had a handful of flour to thicken it . . ."

Hanna did have some flour left over from her baking – not even enough to make a biscuit. Better to let the old liar have it than let it go to waste.

She fetched it from the flour bin. The tramp sifted it into the soup and stirred the pot.

Now there was a sort of smell in the air. Not delicious, exactly, but interesting nonetheless.

"It would be even tastier if I had a little bit of beef and a couple of potatoes," said the tramp with a twinkle in his eye, "but it's no use wishing for things you cannot have."

She had beef and potatoes in the larder. If they helped to flavour the soup, well, who was she to ruin a perfectly good recipe?

The tramp dropped them into the saucepan and stirred the pot slowly, sniffing at the rising steam. "This is going to be fit for a king – only the king would add some cream."

Hanna was on her feet straightaway. She had been saving some cream for her husband's pancakes. "Here," she said, and she poured it into the saucepan herself.

Now the smell from the pot was truly heavenly. The tramp took a spoonful, blew on it to cool it and tasted it. "Perfection!"

The old woman was delighted. She invited the tramp into her house and set the table with her best soup bowls. There was even a drop of wine in the bottle, and some cake for dessert.

"Wonderful," she said, tucking in. "Who would have thought you could make such delicious soup with just a nail?"

The Gift of the Sun

A STORY FROM FINLAND

Imagine a world without fire, where no food can be cooked and the nights are long and cold and dark. That's how it was for the first people on Earth until Jumala, the sky-god, gave them a gift.

Jumala's job was moving the planets around the heavens with his enormous hands. One morning, he was cleaning under his nails with the tip of his sword. A minute piece of the sun had caught under his thumbnail and it fell out. Ilma, the air goddess, caught it in her hands.

"Take care of it for me," called Jumala. "Every speck of sun is precious."

But the spark was too hot for Ilma to hold and she dropped it in a river. Before the water could put out the spark, a small trout gobbled it up. A moment later, the trout was swallowed whole by a salmon, and the salmon ended up as dinner for a monster pike. So there was the little bit of sun, inside a trout, inside a salmon, inside a greedy pike.

Late in the afternoon, a man called Väinämöinen caught the pike for his dinner. He sliced it open and what did he find in its stomach? A whole salmon. He cut the salmon open and what did he discover nestled in that? A little trout. He slit the trout open, and there was the little bit of sun, shining brightly.

Väinämöinen thought it was a glow-worm the trout had swallowed for dinner. He picked it up gently and put it on a twig. "Go on, little one, make good your escape." The spark swelled into flames that ran along the twigs and through all the trees. The forest was on fire; it was as if the setting sun had fallen out of the sky.

Väinämöinen shouted for help. He tried splashing water from the river onto the fire and the flames went out with a sizzle and a hiss. People came to see what was going on, and helped to fetch more water. Soon there was just one small flame left, trapped in an earthenware cup.

"This is a gift from the gods," said Väinämöinen. "We can use it to make life better. But we must be careful with it, too, for it can destroy us as well as help us."

He gave each family a burning twig to carry home, to keep the gift of the sun alive. And that's how fire came to the people, bringing light and warmth to the cold dark night!

The Laziest Boy in the World

A STORY FROM ESTONIA

It was useless for Tiidu's mother to ask him to do anything. He was by far the laziest boy in the world. He wouldn't get out of bed for breakfast, let alone to look for work.

Sometimes he would go outside when it was warm, but only as far as the gate, and then only to sit on the wall, playing a cheap flute.

One day, an old beggar with a dog came along. He stopped by the gate and mopped his brow. He looked sad and Tiidu felt sorry for him.

"Listen to this tune, sir," he said, and began to play.

The song brought a smile to the old man's face. "I remember this old ditty from my childhood, and you play it well. What do you want to be when you grow up?"

"I'm hoping to be rich so I won't have to do anything," said Tiidu.

The old man laughed and his dog wagged its tail. "You cannot be rich unless you work hard."

"That's what my mother says," said Tiidu.

"You put a smile on my face, so here's some advice," said the old man. "You have a knack for playing music. Get yourself a set of bagpipes. People like bagpipes. I am sure you would do

73

well. In fact, I think your talent for music will make you rich." And the old man hobbled off down the road, his dog still wagging its tail.

"Hey!" called Tiidu after him. "Where am I going to get a set of bagpipes?"

But the man didn't reply and Tiidu followed him, shouting. He lost him in the market square in the crowds. What was he to do now? Tiidu stood by the fountain in the square, playing his flute. A couple of passers-by tossed coins in his cap. Imagine that! Tiidu had never earned a penny before. Maybe he could make enough to buy a set of bagpipes one day. He decided to try.

All summer he travelled from town to town, playing his flute at country fairs and village fêtes. People danced to his music and sang along with his songs. Before long, Tiidu could afford a set of bagpipes. He spent all his spare time learning to coax the best sound out of them.

Soon his fame spread across the country. No important christening, marriage or funeral was complete without Tiidu's exquisite music. Lords, ladies and even the king pressed money and gifts on him – velvet cloaks, leather boots, diamond rings and more. The young man was rich beyond his wildest dreams.

After a few years, Tiidu decided to go home, to share his wealth with his family. His mother didn't recognize him when he knocked on the door. His parents couldn't believe their eyes. Their good-for-nothing son was dressed in fine clothes and shaking their hands as if he were gentry.

Hugging his mother, Tiidu saw an old man hobbling past the window with his dog – the very same man who'd given him advice all those years ago. The beggar stopped and doffed his cap, smiling.

"Wait!" Tiidu called, and rushed out to thank him – but by the time he'd opened the door, the old man had vanished again!

The Fighting Fisherman

A STORY FROM LATVIA

Ayoung fisherman named Pastaris liked to sail far into the Baltic Sea in search of large shoals of fish. One evening, as he headed home, the water started bubbling beside his boat and a huge giant rose out of the depths. Before Pastaris could do anything, the giant grabbed hold of him and carried him off to his castle on a remote island.

"Cook for me and look after my castle," commanded the giant. "Work hard and I shall pay you well. There's only one rule you must obey. If you hear anything strange at night, ignore it."

Pastaris thought the rule was very peculiar, but he agreed — what else could he do?

That night, he woke up with a start. Someone was sobbing in the room next door. He lit a candle and went to investigate. A young lady was sitting on the edge of a bed, weeping.

"Who are you?" Pastaris asked.

"The giant kidnapped me," she said. "He wants me to marry him."

Just then, heavy footsteps came along the corridor. "I warned you to obey the rule!" the giant roared, and he hurled Pastaris through the window.

Pastaris flew through the air, and landed in a wilderness far from the Baltic. He walked and walked, looking for a road to take him back. He couldn't stop thinking about the beautiful girl he had left behind him.

After a while, he came across four hunters who were sitting round a fire.

"Help us," said one of the men. "We have killed a bear but we can't divide it fairly."

Pastaris borrowed a sword and cut the bear into four equal parts. Each of the men gave him a gift in return. The first one gave him a hair from a bull's tail. "Hold this in your hand and you will have the strongest punch in the world."

The second handed him a feather. "Tuck this behind your ear, and you will be able to fly at the speed of light."

The third man's gift was a scale from a fish. "Hold this between your finger and thumb, and you will be able to swim faster than any shark."

The last man held out the leg of an ant. "Use it like a spade and it will dig right through to the other side of the world."

With the four gifts in his pocket, Pastaris set off for the castle. After a mile or two, he heard a familiar roar. "Where do you think you're going?" the giant shouted.

Pastaris grasped the bull's hair and punched him. The giant flew through the air.

"Set the girl free, or I'll kill you where you stand," Pastaris shouted.

The furious giant sneered, "I cannot be killed. My soul is hidden where no one can reach it. In my castle is a chest, and inside that chest is a sword that can cut through anything, even the enchanted trees in the wood around my castle. In that wood lives a serpent who guards a white dove. And in the dove's nest is an egg. My soul is inside it. No one has ever been able to find the nest, and, even if they did, they would never be able to crush the egg."

Pastaris took out the fish scale and dived into the sea. In a few strokes, he reached the giant's castle, found the chest and smashed it open. There was the sword! Pastaris hacked through the enchanted wood and found the serpent guarding the dove. He killed it with one blow. The dove, frightened by the noise, took off into the sky. Pastaris grabbed the magic feather and followed, flying on invisible wings.

Across the seven seas went the dove, into a jungle thick with creepers. It settled in a tree so high that no one could ever climb it. Its nest was hidden in the leaves, and in the nest lay the egg. Pastaris swooped down and grabbed it. The egg slipped out of his hands and plummeted to the ground. Instead of smashing, it buried itself deep in the earth.

Pastaris dug into the ground with the ant's leg. When he found the egg, he put the bull's hair in his boot and stamped on it. The giant's dying scream echoed right around the world.

Pastaris used the fish scale to hurry back to the castle and rescue the beautiful girl. She was delighted to marry the brave young fisherman, so everything worked out perfectly!

The Mermaid's Marriage

A STORY FROM LITHUANIA

It was a match made in heaven by Perkunas, the king of the gods himself. Jurate, his own daughter, the mermaid queen of the seas, was to marry Patrimpas, the god of water.

But before she could go to her wedding, Jurate had one more job to do. Kastytis the fisherman had been catching too many fish and she, as protector of the seas, had to stop him.

The fisherman was mending nets when the mermaid surfaced. She had expected an old man, his skin pruned by the Baltic sun. Instead here was a handsome lad, with eyes as deep and blue as the sea itself. The queen of the mermaids was lost for words.

Kastytis looked up from his work in amazement and his awl slipped in his hand.

"You have pricked your finger." Jurate reached out and touched her finger to his. Love blossomed even as her mermaid magic healed the wound.

"Come with me to my castle under the sea. It is all ready for a wedding."

A mermaid's invitation is impossible to refuse. Before he knew it, Kastytis was nodding and spiralling down in Jurate's arms to the depths of the Baltic.

"Here is my palace, made of amber. See, my servants are preparing for the wedding feast," Jurate said.

Mermaids crowded around their mistress, their eyes full of curiosity.

"Your highness, this mortal breathes under water. Is he under your spell?"

"Kastytis is my groom," Jurate replied.

"But, your highness, you are to wed Patrimpas."

"I shall marry a fisherman."

Gods have spies everywhere. Even as Jurate spoke, a kite-fish streaked up to the surface of the Baltic, turning into a white-winged gull as it hit the air, heading for the home of Perkunas, king of the gods.

"My lord, Jurate is marrying a mortal."

"But I promised her to Patrimpas!" Perkunas roared. His face darkened with anger and the sky went as black as lead. How dare his daughter defy her father?

Perkunas had brought Jurate up to be obstinate and determined. She would refuse to leave this fisherman if he asked her to. He would have to think of something else.

A flash of lightning shot out of Perkunas's fingers, knifed through the sea and hit Jurate's amber castle. The walls shattered into a million golden pieces. Kastytis died in Jurate's arms, his heart pierced by a spike of flying amber. Perkunas had won; Jurate would not wed her mortal.

But Jurate refused to marry Patrimpas. If she couldn't have Kastytis, she wanted no one at all.

They say Jurate still lives at the bottom of the Baltic, weeping tears of precious amber. Sometimes fishermen find them in their nets, or on the sands of the Baltic coast, and remember Kastytis and his mermaid love.

The Tsar's Wedding Ring

A STORY FROM RUSSIA

The tsar of Russia lost his wedding ring while out hunting bears. "I shall give a reward to whoever finds it," he announced.

Nikolai was a poor soldier. He was travelling across Russia, returning from a long war. As he trudged through cold woods, he spotted something in the snow. It was the ring! He presented himself at the Winter Palace without delay to claim his reward.

"I'll let you see the king," said the guard, "but only if you promise to split the reward with me. We'll have half each."

Nikolai knew he had no choice. Without the guard's help, he could not hope to see the king.

"Let's write a contract and sign it," he said. "That way you'll be sure to get your share."

The tsar was breakfasting on caviar and blini when Nikolai was announced.

"I have your ring, sire," he said, bowing deeply.

The tsar clapped his hands with delight. "My ring? Well done, sir. What do you want for a reward?"

Nikolai spoke without hesitation. "Ten days in the palace dungeons, sire, with only black bread and water for nourishment."

The tsar was taken aback. The soldier could have asked for anything: caviar, furs,

jewels, or even a treasure-chest full of roubles. But if a spell in the dungeons was what he wanted, that was what he would have.

As Nikolai was being led away, something fluttered out of his back pocket to the floor.

"What's that?" asked the tsar.

"It's a contract between me and your guard," replied Nikolai. "He insisted on it before he would let me see you."

"Half of what you get, eh?" laughed the tsar, reading the paper. "What a greedy fellow! I suggest we let him take all of your reward."

The guard was immediately thrown into prison. And the king, delighted by the soldier's wit, decided to give him a second gift – a chest full of newly minted roubles! Nikolai lived on caviar for the rest of his life.

Thirsty are the Reeds

A STORY FROM HUNGARY

A king was strolling by the river Danube with his advisors.

"Look at those poor reeds," he said. "They need rain badly. The weather's been dry for weeks."

The advisors sniggered behind the king's back. Imagine thinking that reeds in a swamp needed rain! They had their roots in water all the time. The king was really foolish sometimes.

That night, the king invited his advisors to a banquet in the ceremonial hall. "Don't ruin your appetite by snacking beforehand," he said. "Cook is preparing lots of delicious dishes for us."

Even before the dinner gong rang that evening, the king's men had gathered outside the dining hall. The smells from the kitchen were making their mouths water. What delicious treats had the cook dreamed up for them?

The servants showed each man to his place round the grand table. "You each have a bowl of perfumed water under your chair," the head butler announced. "Please cool your feet in it."

Smirking once again, the king's men took off their shoes and put their feet in the bowls. Fancy thinking they needed to keep their feet cool while they ate! But they would humour the foolish king. It was worth it just to have a delicious feast.

The king took his place at the head of the table and the servants brought in the food. As the king had promised, it was absolutely delicious: fish cooked in creamy sauces, roast meats and stews, pies with butter pastry and exotic vegetables cooked with herbs and spices. There was only one thing missing from the table – there was nothing to drink.

"Your majesty," whispered the king's most senior advisor, "if I may be so bold as to point it out, the servants have forgotten the wine."

"They have not forgotten," replied the king loudly so he could be heard all around the table. "I instructed them not to. We are not having wine tonight."

The king's men looked at one another. What was his majesty thinking? How could they eat all this food without drinking anything?

"Perhaps, your majesty," suggested the second most senior advisor, "we would be able to enjoy our food better if someone fetched us a jug of water. Our throats are very dry."

"Nonsense," snapped the king. "You do not need water to drink. Your feet are in bowls full of it."

He looked around the table and smiled. "You all laughed behind my back when I suggested the reeds in the swamp needed rain. You were sure that anything that stood in water didn't need anything to drink. Now you can see for yourselves if you were right or not."

His advisors looked at one another in surprise. It seemed the king was not as foolish as they'd thought – in fact, he was really rather clever!

The Dreadful Dragon

Deep under King Krak's castle, overlooking the river Vistula, there was a huge cavern, home to a vicious dragon. The dragon's hunger could never be satisfied. It always wanted more sheep, more cows, more horses, more goats and more pigs to eat.

And when there were no more animals in the land to be had, it wanted something else. Girls. Plump, delicious girls. Before long there was only one girl left in Kraków: Princess Wanda, the king's own daughter. King Krak was determined not to lose her.

"Offer a reward to any brave knight who kills that wretched dragon," his advisors suggested.

A messenger was sent around the country to read out a proclamation. "Hear ye, hear ye! The king offers his kingdom and Princess Wanda's hand in marriage to the brave nobleman who can rid Kraków of its dragon."

Many brave knights came forward, eager to slay the dragon and marry the princess. But the dragon ate them, bones and all, spitting out their shields and helmets like cherry stones.

Soon there were no more knights to challenge the dragon. The king, in despair, sent another message around the country. Anyone could try to tackle the beast. If they succeeded, whoever they were, they would get the kingdom, along with marriage to the princess.

Only one young man stepped forward – Skuba, the shoemaker's assistant.

"I'll take on the dragon," he said.

"You?" said the king. "You don't look as if you've ever wielded anything heavier than a needle."

"I might not be strong," said Skuba, "but my shoemaker's skills might vanquish the dragon."

The king shrugged. "Try if you like, but I doubt you'll succeed."

It was late in the afternoon; there was not a moment to lose. At sundown the dragon would come out of the cave, bellowing for its dinner.

Skuba bought a dead sheep from the butcher's. He cut the sheep open and packed its empty stomach with sulphur. Then he sewed it up again, as carefully as if he were handling the king's own shoes.

At sunset, the dragon emerged. Its sharp eyes picked out a dead sheep on the grass. It tore the sheep in half with its razor-sharp teeth. There was nothing tastier in the world than fresh meat. But what was this? Something was seeping out of the carcass into the dragon's throat. Something hot – something burning!

The dragon coughed. Its insides were on fire. It tried to spit out the dead sheep but it had slipped down to its stomach already. Water! That would help to put out the fire in its belly. The dragon swooped down to the river Vistula. It started drinking as fast as it could.

It was no use. No use at all. No matter how much water the dragon poured down its gullet, it could not put out the fire in its belly. Faster and faster it drank, churning up the water, swallowing fish and mud and dead gulls. Soon it had swollen to twice its normal size. With a loud pop, it exploded, showering Kraków with rainbow-coloured scales.

How the people cheered! They were safe at last.

Skuba and Princess Wanda fell in love and married soon afterwards, in the cathedral next to the castle. A statue of the dragon was placed nearby to remind everyone how brave Skuba was. It is still there today, glaring at passers-by, its claws raking the air.

Keeping Secrets

A STORY FROM ROMANIA

Dana was a mean old woman who spread vicious rumours and told fibs about people. One day she was out for a walk when she came across a stranger in the fields. Who was he? What did he want in the village? And what was in the sack he was carrying on his back?

"Good morning." The stranger doffed his hat.

"Good morning," Dana replied eagerly. Maybe he would tell her what she wanted to know. It would be fun to gossip about him in the village later.

"I wonder if you could do me a favour," the stranger said politely. "Look after this sack for me, just for a few hours."

The sack seemed to be squirming. Whatever was inside it was alive. Perhaps the stranger was a poacher and had caught a rabbit or a pheasant.

"I don't know if I should," said Dana. "I don't even know who you are."

"I am a magician," the stranger said, and winked at her.

"Really?" The old woman had never met a magician. She'd better do as he asked.

"Please, will you look after the sack for me?" the magician repeated.

"I'll take it, your . . . your magicness," she said. "What's in it?"

"I'm afraid I can't tell you. It's a secret."

Dana bowed her head. "Of course. I understand."

"If you open the sack, you'll get yourself into a lot of trouble," the magician warned her.

She bowed again. When she looked up, the magician had vanished.

Dana hurried home, the sack bouncing on her hunched back. It was surprisingly light. So it couldn't be a rabbit or a pheasant . . . but what could it be?

She set the sack down and inspected it closely. It wasn't fair, the magician not telling her

what she was looking after. Why couldn't he reveal his secret? What was he hiding?

She could hear a faint buzzing coming from the sack. What if whatever was inside it was suffocating? What if it needed air? Dana decided to open the sack, just a fraction. And while she was at it, she might have a look. Surely one little peep couldn't hurt . . .

With trembling fingers, she undid the rope. The buzzing grew louder; the sack started to squirm. Something crawled out of it, and up her arm. A grasshopper! Ugh! The old woman screamed and dropped the rope. Thousands of insects followed the grasshopper — ants, flies, beetles, butterflies, spiders, even wasps! They flew into the old woman's hair, they filled the house, buzzing, squirming, flapping, droning.

She had to get rid of them. Blindly, she reached out to open the window.

"Can I have my sack back, please?" The magician was standing at the window, smiling at her.

"I am sorry — the insects escaped!" Dana cried.

"I told you not to open the sack. You must get them back for me, every single one of them."

"I wish I could, but how?"

"Like this." The magician made a sign, and Dana changed into a woodpecker with a long beak. "You must fly around the world, chasing the insects. Only when my sack is full once more will you become a woman again."

The bird fluttered her wings and flew out of the window. Poor Dana still hasn't completed her task — listen carefully the next time you go to the woods and you might hear the woodpecker hunting feverishly for insects, tapping with its beak on tree trunks, trying to find them all.

Orfeo in the Underworld

A STORY FROM BULGARIA

Orfeo was a man of many talents, gifted in medicine and music. He lived high up in the Rhodope Mountains with his wife, a nymph named Evredika. Orfeo had invented a new musical instrument, the lyre, and every day he played it to celebrate his love for his bride. Orfeo thought that life was perfect and his happiness would last forever.

But it was not so. One day, running across a field, Evredika was bitten by a snake. Orfeo rushed to her side with salves and potions, but he was too late to cure her. Evredika died.

Orfeo was inconsolable. How could he live without Evredika? How could he enjoy sunshine and fresh air when his bride was trapped in the dark and gloomy underworld? There was only one thing to do, he decided — go down to the underworld himself and convince its ruler, Hades, to release Evredika, so he could take her back to the upper world with him.

The dead reach the underworld quickly, their spirits trickling through cracks in the earth like rainwater. Orfeo had to take the long way around. He climbed up a mountain and picked his way down to a gaping hole in a smoking crater at the top. Within it, a long tunnel led to a dark river, the River of Sorrow, where a ferryman waited to carry the dead across, paid with a single coin for every soul.

On the far side, Hades and his wife Persephone sat on golden thrones, welcoming the dead to the underworld. "Make yourselves comfortable, oh ye who have given up on life," Hades boomed.

Stepping off the boat, Orfeo stood out in the crowd of moon-white faces. He bowed. "Your highnesses, if I could have a word with you . . ."

Persephone started, amazed. Here was a man with the glow of life still in his flesh. Why was he in the underworld?

"I am Orfeo of Thrace."

"Orfeo the musician?" Hades' voice echoed round the cavern. "We have heard of your talent for music and medicine."

"Your highnesses, my bride Evredika was taken before her time. I beg you to release her."

Hades' smile changed to a scowl. "No one ever returns from the underworld. The souls of the dead are mine and Persephone's."

"But she is my muse," cried Orfeo. "Without her I cannot compose new songs." And he whipped his lyre from under his cloak and started playing a sad song for Evredika. It was the first time ever that music had echoed around the vast caverns of the underworld. The souls of the dead stopped to listen to the sad, beautiful sound.

Persephone stood up and clasped Orfeo's hand. His music had touched her ice-cold heart. "Perhaps, sire, just this once, we can make an exception."

The crowd of souls parted and Evredika floated to his side, a white shadow wreathed in mist.

Persephone spoke. "She is not yet a ghost. Her flesh will become firm and warm again once you reach the sunlight. But beware, Orfeo, you must not look at your bride again until you both reach the upper world."

"Not until we both reach the upper world." Orfeo started walking, the lyre under his arm. On the banks of the river, he paid the ferryman once more: a coin for him, a coin for Evredika. There was no sound from behind him as he got off the ferry, as his footsteps echoed along the dark tunnel. The souls of the dead whispered to him. "Is your bride really following you or has she been kept in the underworld? Why don't you look back at her?"

Orfeo hurried on. He knew the souls were trying to trick him. Only when he had passed through the gateway and stood bathed in sunshine did he turn.

"Evredika!"

All around him, the invisible souls snickered cruelly. Orfeo had turned too soon. Evredika was still a step from the light, still in the kingdom of Hades. She reached out, trying to grab hold of him, but it was no use. Orfeo had broken Persephone's rule. The darkness swallowed her up and she was gone. Forever.

The Pirates' Punishment

A STORY FROM GREECE

A young man hired a ship to take him from Athens to the Greek island of Naxos, but the crew had other ideas.

"Where shall we really take him?" they sniggered. "Turkey? North Africa? We can get a whole bag of gold for him there."

The seamen looked honest, but they were really pirates. Their job was to kidnap passengers and sell them as slaves, and they made a lot of money doing it.

"The poor fellow is still just a boy," muttered one of the oarsmen. "Won't his mother miss him?"

The others laughed. "Not as much as we'd miss the gold if we let him go!"

The sun was high in the sky when the passenger asked, "Is this really the way to Naxos?"

"We've done this journey many times before, sir," the captain replied.

The oarsmen threw worried glances at each other. Did the young man suspect foul play already?

"I would like some wine, if I may," said the passenger, sniffing the air. "You seem to have some decent stuff on board."

The captain sniffed the air. Strange, there *was* a smell of expensive wine. But his barrels held nothing but cheap stuff, fit only for workmen.

"Our senses must be playing tricks on us, sir. We have been out in the sun too long."

The passenger laughed. "Perhaps, Captain. But tell me, is the sun playing tricks on my eyes too, or have the masts on your ship changed to vines?"

The captain looked up. The straight masts seemed to have warped in the midday heat. They had grown branches covered with leaves. Vine leaves.

"The sun must be hotter than I thought," said the captain. "I'm seeing things."

"I do like a bit of fun," said the passenger. He started dancing. His hair had changed from black to gold, his eyes were the colour of ripe grapes.

Was he a magician? Someone in the crew started to pray. "Oh, Dionysus, god of wine, help us!"

"But I *am* helping you," laughed the passenger, and his golden hair shone even brighter in the sun.

The captain reeled. They had kidnapped a god, the son of Zeus himself. These strange happenings were his punishment for his wickedness and greed.

A scream made him look around. The oars had turned into serpents. "Abandon ship!" he yelled.

The men needed no further prompting, even though none of them could swim very well. In a minute, they were all in the sea, struggling to keep afloat.

"I am the god of happiness, the god of revelry," shouted Dionysus from the deck of the ship. "You mock me by kidnapping people, by turning their lives to misery. I should let you all drown, but one of you spoke kindly about me and my mother, so I shall spare your lives."

He passed his hand over the sea and the pirates suddenly turned into dolphins.

"Go!" ordered Dionysus, "and from now on, be kind to all people crossing the sea. Help them when they are in trouble."

The dolphins swam away, leaping into the air, blessing Dionysus for his forgiveness. To this day, they still roam the wine-dark sea, helping sailors and swimmers in distress.

Green Figs, Purple Figs

A STORY FROM MALTA

A hungry man wandered into a deserted orchard. He spotted a fig tree covered with ripe purple figs. His tummy was rumbling, so he snatched four figs and stuffed them straight into his mouth. They were delicious, as soft as honey.

The man was about to pick a fifth fig when he felt a twitch just above his bottom. He looked around and would you believe it, there was a scaly tail, just like a snake's, growing out of his back!

"Eat some more, why don't you?" jeered a woman's voice from nearby. "But I warn you, the more you eat, the longer your tail will grow."

The man tried to see who was talking to him, but couldn't see anyone. "I'm sorry I stole your figs, kind lady. I gobbled them up without thinking," he called.

The leaves of the fig tree rustled, and an old witch dropped out of the branches. "Hunger makes robbers of us all," she agreed. "Now come with me. There is other fruit in my orchard."

The young man followed the witch to the other end of the orchard, where a second fig tree stood, covered in green figs.

"Help yourself," laughed the witch. "I hope you are still hungry."

The young man was too scared to turn down the witch's offer, so he chose four of the smallest figs and chewed them slowly.

As soon as he finished the fourth one, he felt another twitch and his tail disappeared, just like that!

"You are the only one who has ever apologized for stealing my fruit," said the witch. "Pick as many as you want, young man, and take them with my blessing. They will bring you good luck."

The man picked four green figs, then went back to the first tree and took four purple ones.

Wrapping them up carefully, he set off for the city. He hurried to the market. "Ripe figs for sale! Four figs for a penny! Purple figs that will melt like honey on your tongue!"

The king's daughter happened to be at the market that day, and heard the young man as she passed. "Figs! How delicious," she said, and sent a servant to buy them. But as soon as she ate the figs, she felt a twitch in the small of her back.

"Papa, Papa!"

The king rushed to his daughter's chamber. "What's wrong, Princess?"

"I have a scaly tail, Papa, just like a snake's – look!"

The king was horrified! The royal princess with a horrible tail! He summoned the court physician. The physician sent for the surgeons at the royal hospital. No one could tell the king why the tail had appeared, and no one had the faintest idea how to get rid of it.

In despair, the king sent messengers far and wide, crying, "If there is anyone in the land that can cure the princess, the king will give him a treasure chest full of gold and a casket of diamonds."

The young man set to work at once. He chopped up the four green figs and boiled them with sugar till they turned to fig jam. When the jam was cool, he spooned it carefully into a medicine jar and hurried with it to the king's palace, dressed as a doctor.

"Your majesty, I am sure this rare tincture will rid the princess of her tail. Just one spoonful a day for two weeks should do the trick."

The king agreed. The princess would have one spoonful with her breakfast every morning. Imagine the little girl's joy when, having finished the fig jam, she felt a twitch in the small of her back. "Papa, the tail has gone!" she cried.

The king kept his promise and gave the young man a treasure chest full of gold, and a casket packed with diamonds. He looked for the witch, to share his good luck with her, but he never found her or the enchanted fig trees again.

With the gold and the diamonds, he lived in luxury for the rest of his life. But he never ate another fig!

The Silver Goose

A STORY FROM ITALY

A young count named Carlo hung a sign above the front door of his palace in Genoa.

MONEY CAN GET YOU ANYTHING YOU WANT

The king was intrigued by the statement, and invited Carlo to the carnival ball at his palace. "Can money really get you anything you want?" he asked.

"I believe so, sire," replied Carlo boldly, without hesitation.

"Very well," said the king. "You have three days to speak to my daughter. If you haven't by the end of carnival, I shall send you to the gallows and add your fortune to mine."

The count returned home as pale as the sun in late winter. "I am done for," he sobbed to his old nanny. "The king has locked the princess in a tower and posted guards at every door. There's no way to get to her."

"Give me a bag of gold, sir," said Nanny, "and I'll try to help."

Nanny took the gold to a friend of hers who was a talented silversmith. "Make me a large goose on wheels," she said. "Its beak must open and its tail must wag, and it must lay silver eggs at the touch of a lever. Have it ready by tomorrow."

"I couldn't possibly build such a wonder in a day," said the silversmith.

Nanny scattered the gold on the silversmith's workbench — more than he'd ever seen in his life.

"Hire every other silversmith in Genoa if you need to," she said. "I'll come back for the goose tomorrow at dawn."

With a dozen men working on it, the silver goose was ready on time — it even had a diamond chain to pull it around. Nanny towed it out of the workshop, and through the city streets, where

the carnival had started. It caused an immediate sensation!

"Did you see that amazing silver goose on wheels?"

"It wags its tail most realistically."

"And it lays eggs too. Silver ones, encrusted with diamonds."

The princess got to hear about the goose from her servants. "Father, may I go out to see the wondrous silver goose?" she asked.

"No, Princess. Not today. Not till the end of the carnival."

"But, Papa, the lady with the goose will be gone by then," she sobbed.

The king could not bear to see his beloved daughter crying. "Then I shall make the lady bring the goose to the tower."

The princess clapped her hands when the door opened and the silver goose sailed in on its four wheels. "How beautiful it is, how wonderful!"

Things got even more wonderful when the goose split in two. Out of it stepped Carlo, resplendent in his carnival costume.

"Who are you?" the princess asked.

"A young man whose fate lies in your hands," Carlo said sorrowfully. He described the sign he had rashly hung above his door, and the bet he had made. "Tell the king that you spoke to me, and my life will be spared."

The princess beamed. "I'll do more than spare your life. I shall demand to marry you!"

Just then the clock struck midnight, marking the end of the carnival. The king hurried to the tower to celebrate winning his bet. Imagine his surprise when he saw the princess kissing Carlo! He was dumbfounded. "I was wrong, then. Money *can* get you anything you want."

But Carlo shook his head. "No, I was wrong. Money might help, but you also need brains, passion, hard work, a nanny with a clever plan – and a little bit of good luck!"

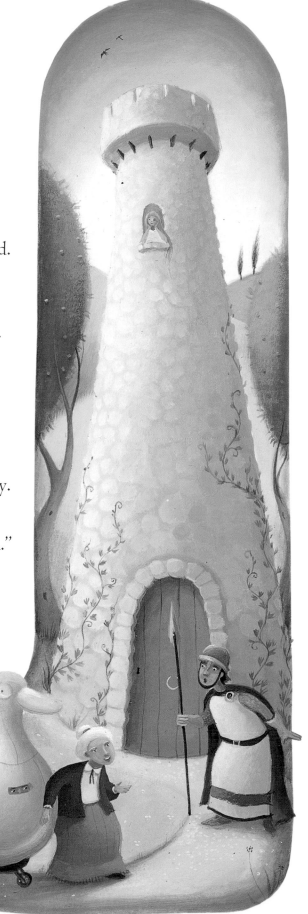

The Herdsman's Song

From his little hut high up in the Alps, Res could see his village in the valley below — windows glowing with warm light, people scurrying home along the main street. Was his bride-to-be among them? Was she missing him? Res had been hired to mind cattle on the mountain pastures all summer — a terribly long time for him to be away from his girl.

The clock in the steeple struck seven. That meant bedtime for Res, who went to work before dawn. He retired to the loft.

In the middle of the night, a noise woke him up. He lifted his head. Was it a cow mooing, or mice scuttling across the kitchen floor in search of cheese? Res opened the loft door a crack.

Three men were sitting by the hearth, their shadows spread like rugs behind them. But what strange men they were, tall as giants yet pale as ghosts. One of them was throwing sticks on the fire. A second was stirring milk in the copper pan. The third was unwrapping something with care.

It was a musical instrument, a long horn that was narrow at one end but widened to a bell shape at the base. The willowy giant carried it outside and a moment later haunting music filled the air. Res had never heard anything like it. It was joyous and sad at the same time; it made him think of his bride-to-be, far below.

The sound of the horn was accompanied by the jangle of cowbells. The herd had gathered around the player. The animals too seemed to be under the spell of the music.

The milk in the copper pan frothed up and boiled. One of the strangers ladled it into three bowls. "Herdsman, don't be frightened," he called. "Come and have some milk. You may drink out of any bowl you choose."

The strangers had known all along that Res was watching! Slowly, he climbed down the ladder. Outside, the music stopped and the third stranger came in with the horn.

"Choose this one, lad," said the stranger who had been stoking the fire. He held out one of the bowls and Res could see that the milk in it had turned bright red. "It will make you as strong as a bull, as fast on your feet as a lynx."

"No, take this one," said the second stranger, offering the second bowl. The milk in it had turned green. "This will bring you untold wealth. You will strike gold in the mountains."

The third stranger picked up the last bowl, the milk in it still as white as the snow on the mountain peaks. "Take this, my lad, and I will leave you the gift of my music, the alp-horn."

Res hesitated. He wanted to be strong; he wanted to find treasure and be rich. Then he thought of the stranger's haunting song and his bride in the valley below, waiting to hear from him.

He drank the white milk.

The strangers applauded. "Had you taken one of the other bowls, we would have had to keep the alp-horn for another hundred years. But now it belongs to you, to the people of the mountains."

The strangers moved to the door and waved farewell. Outside, there was a rush of wind, and they were gone.

Res picked up the alp-horn, surprised that it was taller than him. He took it outside and held it to his lips again, blowing gently. Haunting music echoed around the mountains. The herd gathered around him, mooing to the magical sound of the alp-horn. It was music that would become the sound of the Alpine herdsman, filling the mountains with its beauty forevermore.

The Frog's Wedding

A STORY FROM AUSTRIA

A dairy farmer and his wife went for a walk in the hills and found a small frog in the edelweiss. "I've always wanted a daughter," said the woman. "I'll raise this frog as my own child and call her Katharina."

The little creature thrived in the farmer's house. She learnt to speak, to read and even to sing. Her voice was so beautiful that everyone loved to listen to her.

One afternoon, a prince happened to ride past the cottage. He heard the frog singing through her bedroom window and fell under her spell immediately.

"Is that your daughter I hear?" he asked the farmer, who was churning butter on the doorstep. "May I speak to her?"

"Alas, Katharina sees no one," replied the farmer.

"But I have fallen in love with her," insisted the prince. "I want to make her my wife."

The farmer wiped his hands on a cloth. "I'll see what she thinks."

The frog knew in her heart of hearts that she could never marry the prince. But she wondered what it would feel like to be a bride, to see inside a palace — maybe even to be kissed. So she said yes, on one condition: that the prince didn't see her before the wedding — not even on the day itself. He would see her at the altar and not a minute sooner.

A mystery bride! thought the prince excitedly, and he accepted Katharina's one condition straightaway.

On the day of the wedding, the farmer's wife dressed Katharina in a wedding gown made of paper, and the bride set out in a toy carriage pulled by a rooster, singing as she drove. As she came closer to the palace the little frog started to feel a bit nervous. She hoped the prince wouldn't mind the trick she'd played on him.

At a bend in the road, Katharina passed three fairies who were on their way to the wedding. One of them was coughing violently; she had gone purple in the face. Her companions were frantically thumping her on the back.

"Help! Help!"

The frog stopped the carriage. "What's the matter?"

"Our friend has a fishbone stuck in her throat."

The third fairy tried to speak, but she couldn't. The sight of a frog in a wedding gown was too much for her. The violent coughing turned to gales of giggles — which dislodged the fishbone.

"Why," said the first fairy, "you have saved our companion's life. Such kindness deserves a great reward." She waved her wand and the toy carriage turned into a real one, pulled by six white horses.

"Here is my reward," said the second fairy. She pointed her wand at the wedding dress and the paper turned to silk and lace.

"I owe you the greatest reward of all," said the third fairy. She sprinkled gold dust in the air, chanting a spell. Instantly Katharina turned into a beautiful young woman, her eyes sparkling with joy and gratitude.

The church bells were pealing as the carriage stopped outside the palace. Footmen rushed to open the door and the only person happier than Katharina that day was the handsome prince who married her.

The Dwarf's Gift

A STORY FROM GERMANY

Hans worked hard down the mine to support his large family. But then he fell ill – too ill even to raise his head from the pillow.

"Mother," called his eldest son, "can we call the doctor? Papa has a fever."

Anna, the miner's wife, sighed. "We have not a penny left in the house, son. With your papa not working, there's been no money coming in and we have sold everything we have, even my dearest possession." She rubbed the pale mark on her finger where her wedding ring used to be.

"But there must be something we can do!" insisted the boy.

"I will go to the forest," said Anna. "I'll collect a basket of fir cones for you to sell at the market. It might pay for a visit from the doctor."

Anna put on her patched cloak and slipped out into the rain. She took a large basket with her. When she came across a fir tree, she started filling it with cones that had fallen off the branches.

"A fine night for stealing fir cones, madam. They belong to me and only I may pick them."

The loud voice made Anna jump. She looked around to see a dwarf beside her, his long beard spangled with raindrops.

"I didn't mean to steal, kind sir. I didn't know this tree belonged to anyone."

The dwarf smiled at her. "No one has ever called me kind or a sir before. Tell me, why do you need fir cones?"

Anna told the dwarf about her poor, sick husband. He listened kindly, then said, "Go further up the hill and you will find another fir tree. Its cones will fetch a bit more at the market than these ones."

Anna thanked the dwarf and stumbled on, her shoes slipping on the wet ground. As the dwarf had promised, she found another fir tree. Its branches seemed to reach out from one end of the hill to the other. Breathless, Anna sat underneath it to rest, her basket by her side. Suddenly the wind shook the mighty tree, and a torrent of fir cones rained into the basket.

Anna jumped up. Not one fir cone had fallen on her, only in the basket. "Why, thank you, tree!" And she hurried back home.

The children were still awake, waiting for her in the kitchen. "Did you bring the fir cones, Mama?"

She set the basket down on the table. "Plenty of them."

"Why, Mama, look!"

Anna stared at the basket. Every single cone had turned to silver, pure silver.

Early the next day, she went to see the silversmith in town. He paid her a tidy sum of money for the two cones she took with her, enough to call the doctor and buy medicine for her husband. Before long, he was well enough to return to the mines.

Not that he needed to, of course. The rest of the cones fetched enough money to make Hans and his family rich. Word of their good luck soon got around, and many searched for the dwarf and the magic fir tree, but no one ever found them.

"The dwarf will only show himself when he chooses," said Hans. "He is Gubich, the king of the dwarves."

To this day, some people in Germany keep silver fir cones in their houses for luck.

Hans, the Hero of Haarlem

A STORY FROM HOLLAND

It was a bitterly cold evening. "Thank your mother for the biscuits," Hans's uncle called from the doorway of his cottage.

"I will," said Hans, knotting his scarf tightly and hurrying off. His mother was making fried cakes for dinner, so he didn't want to be late. Besides, it was getting dark.

Like many parts of Holland, Haarlem was built on marshy land reclaimed from the sea. There were thick walls around it to keep the water at bay, and windmills to pump the water back along the canals if the tide rose too high. Hans had heard horrible stories about other cities being flooded, but he didn't believe it could ever happen in Haarlem. The walls were too strong.

Hans's tummy was rumbling so loudly with hunger that he nearly didn't hear the faint splash of water as he hurried along beside the dyke.

Yet something his teacher had said in class made him stop. *A flood always starts with a trickle, children.*

That's what Hans had heard. A trickle of water running down stone. He started looking for it. It wasn't easy in the twilight but he found it, bubbling out of a crack between two stones. For a moment he thought of running home to fetch his father, or one of the men who maintained the dykes and canals. But even as he watched, the water seemed to gush more strongly.

Hans knew he had to plug the hole. But with what? He had nothing with him, nothing except his scarf, and that would be no good.

"Help!" he shouted. "It's an emergency! Someone, help."

No one answered. The road was deserted.

Hans started to panic. It would be his fault if he left and the sea broke the wall down, flooding Haarlem. What could he do?

Suddenly Hans had an idea. He stuck his finger in the hole, stopping the flow of water. Now all he had to do was wait until someone passed by.

Hans waited and waited. No one had appeared by midnight. His finger grew numb in the hole, his arm ached and he started to shiver.

"Someone, help!" he called, but no one answered.

The moon came out, turning the world silver. The numbness spread all over Hans's body. He wondered if he would die of cold. A favourite song of his mother's came to mind and he started singing to himself. He had to keep awake somehow, he had to keep his finger in the wall . . . he had to . . .

"Hans?" Someone was wrapping a warm cloak around his shoulders, rubbing his hair. It was his mother.

"Hans, we have been searching for you. Papa and I were very worried."

"The sea was coming in . . ." whispered Hans, and his eyes closed again.

"I know, Hans. The canal man is coming. You've saved the city from a terrible flood."

"A flood always starts with a trickle," mumbled Hans, and the hero that saved Haarlem fell into his mother's arms, exhausted.

The Lacemakers of Bruges

A STORY FROM BELGIUM

"Ugh," cried Old Martha, waving her duster. "There's a spider behind the wardrobe."

"Don't hurt it," said Agnes. "Spiders are harmless, and I don't want anyone to be sad or hurt today."

Today was a very special day for Agnes. She and Old Martha were cleaning the house because Agnes's papa was coming home after a long journey at sea. Agnes had already spotted his ship from the bedroom window, coming slowly up the canal that connected Bruges, their city, to the sea.

"Put it outside, then," said Old Martha.

Agnes cupped her hand gently around the spider and took it out to the garden. The little creature was just scuttling away when a man in a dark coat appeared at the garden gate.

"Is this Mr Pieter's house?"

"Yes, it is."

"Is your mother home? I need to speak with her at once."

Something in the sailor's manner made Agnes think he brought bad news. She took him to her mother straightaway, and as she closed the door behind her, she heard him start to speak.

"Something terrible has happened . . . "

With those few words, Agnes's world turned upside down. Papa had died at sea. Now she and Mama had no one to look after them and nothing to live on. They had to give up the beautiful house by the canal. They sold most of their furniture and all of their nice clothes. Old Martha helped them find rooms on the edge of town, where Agnes and Mama could try to earn their living making lace.

But a lot of other people in Bruges made lace, people who had far more experience than

Agnes and her mama and could turn out far better lace. Agnes couldn't sell anything that they made to the shopkeepers she approached in town.

"What you need is a new lace pattern to make your work stand out," advised Old Martha. "One that will catch the ladies' eyes."

But where would they find a new pattern? Agnes lay under the apple tree outside their new home and tried to think. She would never give up hope . . .

The wind rustled the branches overhead and something floated down from the tree to land on the cloak Agnes had spread out beside her. It was gossamer from a spider's web. Agnes looked up into the tree. There were spiders up there, letting bits of their web slip away on the breeze.

One by one, the pieces of gossamer floated down to join the first piece on Agnes's cloak. Lying there, white on black, they made a pretty pattern – one that would make a gorgeous piece of new lace, Agnes realized, gazing at it in amazement. Were the spiders rewarding her for saving the spider's life?

Agnes picked up the cloak gently and carried it indoors. "Look, Mama. Isn't this a beautiful pattern?"

Old Martha joined them, and they started working the bobbins right away, copying the pattern in the spider's web. By morning they had a fantastic piece of lace to show the shopkeepers in town, one that no one in Bruges had ever seen before.

"It's perfect for a lady's wedding dress," said the first shopkeeper they approached the moment he saw it. He paid for it right there and then, and ordered more.

From then on, Agnes, Mama and Old Martha never lacked for money again. Soon they had a new house, new clothes, and a new life – all thanks to the little spider that Agnes had saved so long ago.

The Miller's Son

A STORY FROM FRANCE

A miller had three sons. When he died, the eldest inherited the mill and a cornfield. The middle brother was given a donkey. The youngest son, Pierre, got nothing but the granary cat.

"What use is a cat?" Pierre asked. "I'd rather have a cornfield or a donkey."

"Give me your boots and a leather bag," said the cat, "and I'll bring you a fortune."

The miller's son handed over his boots and the leather bag.

The cat put a carrot in the bottom of the bag and hid it in the grass. Before long a rabbit came along and, sniffing out the carrot, hopped into the bag.

"Got you!" said the cat, who'd been watching from behind a bush, and he pounced on the bag.

Later that afternoon, he presented himself to the king, wearing the leather boots.

"Your majesty, the Marquis of Carabas sent me to give you this rabbit as a gift."

"The Marquis of where?" asked the king.

"Carabas," said the cat, with a bow.

"Thank him for me," said the king, who was somewhat surprised but quite delighted to be given such a lovely present.

The next day, the cat returned to the palace with two plump partridges. "Your majesty, the Marquis of Carabas sent me to give you another gift."

"How generous!" said the king. "Please tell him that if he ever visits the city, I'd like to meet him, to thank him personally for his gifts."

The cat hurried home to the miller's son and said, "Tomorrow afternoon, you must go and bathe in the river by the great oak tree. The king's carriage will pass by on its way from the palace to parliament. Do as I say, and you'll make your fortune as I promised. But remember, don't say a word until I tell you to."

While Pierre was swimming, the cat hid his threadbare clothes in the bushes. When he heard the king's coach rattling along the road, he jumped out in front of it and started shouting.

"Help! Help!"

The royal coach stopped at once. "Look!" said the king to his daughter. "It's the cat who brought me the rabbit and the partridges!"

"Sire," panted the cat, "my master the Marquis of Carabas was attacked on his way to see you at the palace. The robbers took his clothes and made off with his coach. I'm afraid the terrible shock means that he won't be able to speak for a while."

"Fetch some new robes from the palace," the king ordered his servants. When they brought the robes, Pierre came out of the river, dried off and got dressed in fine clothes fit for a prince. Then he climbed into the royal carriage right next to the princess.

"Sire," said the cat, "the robbers might be lying in wait for you. Why don't you take a different route to parliament? I'll show the coachmen the way."

So the royal carriage turned off the main road and took a country path through the hills. The miller's cat ran ahead of it, till he saw some men ploughing a field.

"Tell the king this land belongs to the Marquis of Carabas," he shouted, "and I'll come back tomorrow and give each of you a handful of gold."

When the king saw the men working in the field, he rolled down the carriage window.

"Tell me, who owns this land?" he asked them.

"The Marquis of Carabas," they replied, thinking of the gold. The king was impressed.

Further along the track, the king saw women picking fruit in an orchard.

"Tell me, ladies," he asked, "who owns this orchard?"

"The Marquis of Carabas," they chorused. The cat had bribed them too!

"You are a wealthy fellow, sir," the king said to the miller's son.

Remembering the cat's instructions, Pierre just nodded.

Meanwhile the cat had hurried on until he came to a magnificent castle. He knocked on the door and who should answer but the master himself. He was a fearsome ogre who owned all the land the king's carriage was rattling through.

"Good afternoon," said the cat to the ogre. "I have heard that the owner of this castle can turn himself into any kind of creature."

"And what of it?" snarled the ogre.

"Well, sir, I have travelled all around the world and never have I met someone who can change his shape at will. To be honest, I don't believe it."

"Really?" the ogre said, laughing. And he changed himself into a lion.

The cat got such a fright, he leapt up a tree, leaving his boots behind.

"That is most impressive," he said to the ogre, regaining his composure. "But lions are almost as big as ogres. I don't believe you could shrink to be something really small, such as a mouse."

"Of course I can," boomed the ogre. And, twitching his whiskers, he turned himself into a mouse. Instantly the cat jumped down and gobbled him up.

Just then, the royal carriage drew up outside the castle. "Who owns this magnificent pile?" the king asked the cat.

"The Marquis of Carabas, of course," the cat replied.

The king asked if he could look inside, and the cat showed him around. The ogre's servants, who were overjoyed that their horrible master had been destroyed, fetched tea for the princess and Pierre. Neither had as much as a sip. The princess had fallen in love with the miller's son as soon as he had sat next to her, and the miller's son had felt his heart beat like a drum the moment he had laid eyes on the princess.

The king, most impressed with the marquis's estates, agreed that the two should marry. So the cat's promise came true. He really did bring the miller's son a fortune – and a wife to boot!

A Helpful Friend

A fox and a goose were close friends, amigos. The goose wasn't a very clever bird, but the fox was as cunning as the winter night was long.

The goose had inherited a large field, but she didn't use it for anything. One day, she had an idea. She asked the fox, "Will you help me grow wheat in my field? We'll share the harvest."

"That's a splendid idea," said the fox.

The goose fetched a bag of seeds. "Here," she said, "help me sow them, amigo."

"I'd love to," said the fox, "but I'm visiting my cousin today. She's just had cubs."

The goose sowed all the seeds herself, scattering them in the field with her wings. The field was very big, and there were lots of seeds. By the end of the day, the poor goose was exhausted and her wings ached.

When the seedlings started to grow, the goose went to see the fox again. "Amigo, we must water the wheat every morning."

"I know," said the fox, "but I read to my old aunt every morning. She's bedridden, poor thing. Sorry, but I can't help."

So the goose had no choice but to water the seedlings on her own, carrying the bucket by the handle in her beak. It took her a long time to water the whole field, and by the end of the day her neck was very sore.

When the wheat was higher than the goose's head, she went to see the fox once again.

"Our crop is coming along nicely," she said, "but weeds are choking it. Will you help me pull them up?"

"I can't touch weeds, I'm afraid," said the fox. "They make my paws itch."

107

So the poor goose had to tackle the job all by herself. By the time she finished, her feet were sore, there was dust in her feathers and her wings felt as if they were falling off!

But slowly the wheat ripened in the warm sun, and soon it was time to bring in the harvest.

The goose went to see the fox once more. "It's time for us to gather the wheat," she said. "Will you help me?"

"I'm not feeling well," said the fox. "I'm so sorry, but I really can't help."

Poor goose! She had to fetch the sickle and harvest the wheat all by herself. It took her all week to do it. She was worried about the fox too. What was wrong with him?

Her other friend, the greyhound, found her roosting on a fence, looking upset. Her feathers were all ruffled and dirty from her hard work in the field.

"What's the matter?" asked the greyhound.

"I'm so worried about the fox. He couldn't even help me to gather the harvest, because he is ill," the goose honked.

"He's not ill," said the greyhound. "I saw him earlier. He went to the fiesta with his friends."

The goose couldn't believe her friend. "Why would the fox leave me to harvest our wheat on my own?"

"Tell me the whole story," said the greyhound, who quickly saw what the fox had been doing when the goose described all of the excuses he had made.

"I'm afraid that fox isn't to be trusted," said the greyhound. "I'm sure he's going to try to trick you out of your share of the wheat too."

The goose got into a flap. "Ay, ay, ay," she honked. "Whatever shall I do?"

"Tie your wheat up in sheaves," said the greyhound, "and let me hide in one of them. I'll sort that fellow out."

The goose gathered the wheat in sheaves and stood them, one by one, in the barn. Then she left a message for the fox, telling him where she had stored their wheat.

When the fox returned from the fiesta, he found the goose's note. What good news! All that lovely wheat, and he hadn't had to lift a paw to get it. He decided to go and count the

number of sheaves while he thought of a way to convince the goose to give him her share. He headed to the barn, whistling as he went. The fox was still in a holiday mood.

"My, my, my!" he said, admiring the tall sheaves, "this is a fine harvest, to be sure." And he started dancing around the barn, singing at the top of his voice:

> *Look at all this! Isn't it fine!*
> *The wheat is gathered, and it's mine, mine, mine.*

As the fox capered around the barn, something hidden in one of the sheaves caught his eye. It was large and round, like a . . . like a . . .

"A grape," said the fox, and he reached out to pick it.

"I'm afraid it's not ripe yet," boomed a stern voice. And with that, the grape disappeared, because it was really the greyhound's eye, watching the fox. In a flash, the huge dog jumped out of his hiding place in the wheat. He chased the fox round and round the barn. The fox howled and growled and his fur stood on end, because foxes are terrified of greyhounds.

At last the fox dodged around the greyhound and made it to the door. He shot through it faster than a rocket on fiesta night. From that day forth, he never bothered the goose again. She was able to enjoy all the proceeds from her hard work, thanks to her true friend, the greyhound!

Roast Cockerel

A STORY FROM PORTUGAL

A traveller was on a long journey through Portugal and Spain, on his way to Santiago de Compostela. He had been walking for a long time and his feet were killing him. A pedlar passed by on a cart, and the traveller hailed him.

"Where are we, brother?"

"On the outskirts of Barcelos."

After all that walking, the traveller was still in Portugal. He decided to stop under a tree for the night. Tucked up in his travelling cloak, he soon fell asleep.

"Get up!"

Someone was shaking him roughly – a guard in uniform, with two others beside him. The traveller sat up.

"We have orders to search your bag, sir."

The traveller handed the bag over without a murmur. There was nothing in it except for two pieces of flint which he used to make his camp fires.

"I am a traveller on my way to Compostela."

The guard who'd been looking in his bag slung it over his shoulder. "You must come with us, sir. Do not attempt to escape, or we'll have to use force."

Use force? What did they think he was – a dangerous criminal on the run? He'd done nothing wrong.

Standing in a crowded court the next day, he soon found out what they wanted. Someone had stolen a silver cross from a local manor. Searching for the culprit, the police had found him. What was he doing hiding under a tree if he was innocent?

"I wasn't hiding," protested the traveller. "I was just resting."

But it was useless to protest. The police wanted to pin the crime on someone and he was a stranger, a perfect scapegoat with no one to defend him.

The judge stood up to pass sentence. "Stealing is a terrible crime. I must give you the harshest sentence I can. You will be taken to the main square of the town and hanged by the neck until you die. Now clear the courtroom. I must get home to dinner. My roast cockerel will be getting cold."

That stupid judge cared more for his stomach than for justice. Couldn't he see that the real culprit was going free, that an innocent victim was taking his place on the gallows?

"Your honour!" the traveller shouted above the din of the crowd, "I have no alibi, no witness to prove that I did not commit the crime I am accused of. But if I am innocent, let the roast cockerel you are about to eat raise its head and crow."

The crowd burst out laughing. Imagine, a roast cockerel able to crow! The traveller was mad.

People rushed from the courtroom to the main square where the gallows were set up. The executioner put the noose round the traveller's neck. A priest chanted a final blessing.

"May God have mercy on your soul . . . "

"Stop! The man is innocent." The judge was leaning out of his dining-room window at the other end of the square. "The rooster in my dish opened its beak and crowed three times."

The traveller was set free and given a bag of gold to make up for his ordeal. Since then, people across Portugal have kept plaster cockerels in their kitchen to remind them of that fortunate traveller.

A Sleeve in the Soup

A STORY FROM TURKEY

Nasreddin Hodja was a fool, a trickster. His family loved him, but they lived in fear of being shown up in public. Who knew what foolish things Nasreddin would do next? Once, he arrived at his niece's wedding in a tattered robe.

"You can't come in dressed like that," said the best man, who was at the door, welcoming people. "The other guests will think that you intend to bring disrespect on the family."

"But I didn't have time to change," protested Nasreddin. "I wanted to write a poem in honour of the bride and groom and it took longer than I expected."

The best man borrowed a clean robe from the bride's father and gave it to Nasreddin. "Go upstairs and put this on," he hissed, "and make sure no one sees you before you get out of those filthy rags, or you'll bring shame on us all."

After the ceremony, the guests sat down to the wedding feast.

"Please, eat as much as you want," the groom urged everyone, pointing to a table piled high with food.

"Thank you," said Nasreddin in a loud voice, making sure that all the guests could hear him.

He took the lid off the soup bowl and dipped his sleeve in it.

"Eat, my robe, eat," he said.

"What are you doing, Nasreddin?" asked the groom.

"Sir, when I got here in my work clothes, I was nearly turned away," replied Nasreddin. "But now that I am well-dressed, I have been invited to eat as much as I want. It is obvious that you invited this robe to the wedding and not me. I am, therefore, giving it its fair share of the wedding feast."

And everyone in the room marvelled at the fool's wisdom.

Africa

Counting Chickens

A STORY FROM EGYPT

A poor young man named Farouk spent his last few piastres on some eggs. On his way home from the market he stopped to cool his feet in the Nile.

"When these eggs hatch, I'll have twelve chickens," he said to himself. "When they grow up, I'll sell their eggs and make a good bit of money, which I'll invest in a goat. That way I'll sell both eggs and milk. I might even start making cheese. I could have my own stall at the market. The ladies will flock to me for goods and I might choose one of them to be my wife."

Farouk had it all planned: with the money from his market stall, he would buy grain and rice. Then he would sell the grain for bread and beer.

When he got tired of buying and selling grain, Farouk would invest in land. He could buy some houses and rent them out. He could purchase some camels, too — visitors to Egypt paid good money to ride camels to the pyramids.

The young man started pacing up and down. He could see his glorious future stretching out before him: lots of people working for him, farmers renting his land. He would build himself a nice house with a fountain in the courtyard and keep Arab horses for his sons to ride!

When he got old, he would sit outside a café drinking coffee with his friends, playing backgammon and smoking a water pipe encrusted with gems. He wouldn't have to do any work at all. He'd have servants to do everything for him. All he would have to do was enjoy himself, just like the pharaohs of old.

Totally absorbed in thoughts of the comforts that lay in store for him, Farouk sat down without looking — on the basket of eggs. Every single one of them was smashed. Poor Farouk had egg yolk all over his bottom and his dreams lay in smithereens on the ground. He'd learnt a valuable lesson, though: look after the present and let the future take care of itself!

The King's Best Friend

A STORY FROM TUNISIA

The king of Tunisia's best friend was a clown named Mahboul. No one could tell jokes or spin stories better than Mahboul. His only flaw was that he ate too much. The king worried that one day his friend would burst! He decided to teach Mahboul a lesson.

The king invited all his friends to a banquet at the palace, with Mahboul as the guest of honour. The cook was instructed to prepare all of Mahboul's favourite dishes.

The first course was mouth-watering grilled fish with roast peppers. Mahboul was about to tuck in when the king said, "Mahboul, tell us about the man who bought a camel for his son."

That joke was the longest one Mahboul knew. By the time he reached the end, juggling fruit all the while to entertain his audience, the servants had whisked the fish course away. Mahboul wanted to cry with disappointment. He so loved fish with roasted peppers. But here were servants returning from the kitchen with the second course: lamb stew and couscous. It was Mahboul's favourite dish! He would have a double helping to make up for not having any fish.

But – "Mahboul, sing us that song you learnt from the nomads in the desert," ordered the king.

Poor Mahboul had no choice but to sing! The song was longer than the camel joke. By the time he was done, the lamb stew was all gone. Not a bite of meat or a crumb of couscous was left.

By now the clown was ravenous. The servants carried in trays of baklava and honey cakes and Mahboul grabbed handfuls of them.

"Mahboul," said the king, "do some conjuring while we have our dessert."

The clown performed an elaborate trick with his turban. He pulled flowers out of people's ears. While Mahboul was producing doves from the king's sleeves, the table was cleared. The king rose to his feet, signalling that dinner was over, but Mahboul had not had a single morsel.

The king laughed. "You see, Mahboul, you can have fun without gorging yourself on food."

As the king was talking, a messenger came in with grave news of a rebellion in the south. The king retreated at once to a chamber with his advisors, leaving orders that no one was to disturb him.

The king had hardly sat down when there was a knock on the door. It was Mahboul.

"Sire," he said, "I thought I should tell you that I got that joke about the camel wrong. The proper ending is . . . " And he retold the whole joke.

Had anyone but Mahboul interrupted the meeting, the king would have sent them to the gallows at once. But Mahboul was allowed out of the chamber without even a warning.

The war council continued, only to be interrupted a second time. It was Mahboul again.

"Sire, I didn't sing that desert song properly during dinner. This is how it should go . . . " And Mahboul sang the long song all over again.

The king was furious. He waved Mahboul out of the room and returned to the meeting.

But once again Mahboul interrupted the proceedings. "Sire, I forgot to show you my new trick."

The king rose angrily. "How dare you? Do you want to be sent to the gallows?"

"I've heard that people on their way to the gallows are given a sumptuous last meal," Mahboul replied. "I've had nothing to eat tonight, so it sounds tempting."

Then the king realized how cruel he had been. The poor clown was so hungry, he was willing to pay for a meal with his own head!

He ordered the cook to make a sumptuous dinner for Mahboul, and he never tried to teach his best friend a lesson again!

The Lion's Dinner

Two pedlars were returning home from the market in Rabat. A camel-herder at the city gate nodded to them. "Be careful crossing the desert. I've seen lion poo on the ground."

"That can only mean there's a hungry lion roaming the scrubland," said the first pedlar, a bead-seller. "Let's use the mountain road, brother. It might take longer to get home, but it'll be safer."

"I promised my daughter I'd get her some honey cakes from the market," replied his friend, who dealt in pots. "She goes to bed at sundown, so I'll take my chances and cross the plain."

The two pedlars parted ways, the first heading to the mountains, the second clanking across the desert with his pots and pans. Soon he heard a roar in the bushes and a lion leapt into his path.

"Say your last prayers! I am hungry," the lion growled.

"You'll get no sustenance eating me," said the pedlar. "I am only skin and bones."

"I'm not eating you for nourishment," snarled the lion. "I have a headache and a djinn told me only a human brain can get rid of it."

"You're out of luck, then," said the pedlar. "I have no brains in my head at all."

The lion narrowed his eyes. "No brains?"

"A camel-herder warned me about you. If I had any brains, would I have come across the scrubland? No, I would have gone through the mountains."

The lion yawned hungrily. "You might be right. I'll try my luck in the mountains." And he bounded away, leaving the pedlar to get home safely with his daughter's precious honey cakes.

Secrets Are Hard to Keep

A STORY FROM THE SUDAN

One day, as Niel was strolling down the road, he spotted a snake trapped between two rocks. Niel hated seeing a creature in trouble. He pulled the rocks apart carefully, so the snake could slither away.

"I owe you a reward," said the snake. "Hold out your hand." And the snake dropped a snake tooth into his palm.

"Wear it round your neck," he whispered, "and you'll understand everything that animals say. But if you reveal your secret, the charm won't work any more."

"I won't tell anyone," Niel assured him.

The snake flicked out his tongue. "Beware! Secrets are hard to keep, my friend."

That night, lying on the cot next to his wife, Niel heard mice scurrying across the floor.

"Will we find any injera bread in this hut, I wonder?" one mouse squeaked at the other.

Niel sat up in surprise, clasping his charm. He could understand the mouse's squeaking.

"The people in this house never put food away properly," replied the second mouse. "We are going to feast like emperors."

Niel couldn't help laughing. The poor mice would be disappointed. He and his wife had eaten everything.

"Why are you laughing, Niel?" asked his wife.

"I can't tell you," replied Niel, remembering the snake's warning.

In the morning, a milk-seller knocked on the door of the hut.

"I hope these people aren't fools enough to part with their money," Niel heard one goat say to another. "The master has watered down the milk."

Niel laughed out loud again. Being able to understand animals seemed to have a lot of benefits.

"What's the big joke?" asked his wife. "Why can't you tell me?"

"I have my reasons," answered Niel. And he refused to say anything else.

Later that afternoon, Niel's old aunt came to visit, riding on her big cow.

"It's not fair, that woman riding on me in this heat," the cow complained to a stray cat. "She's heavier than a cartload of mangoes."

Niel tried hard not to giggle. Aunt Sora would be furious if she found out what the big cow was saying about her!

"I've had enough!" fumed his wife. "If you don't tell me what's making you laugh, I'm going home to my parents."

Niel didn't want to lose his wife — he loved her too much. He told her his secret immediately, but his wife didn't believe him.

Niel gave her the charm. "Here, you try it."

But the charm had stopped working. Niel's wife couldn't understand what the animals were saying, and when he put the charm around his neck again, neither could Niel. The fun was over!

A few days later, Niel was resting under the mango tree when the snake slithered past.

"I see you have revealed your secret, my friend."

"I did it for my wife." said Niel ruefully.

"True love ought to be rewarded," said the snake. "Put your hand out again."

The snake gave Niel a feather. "Wear it round your neck," he said, "and you will be able to understand everything birds say. But do not reveal the secret to anyone or the charm will stop working."

"I've learnt my lesson," said Niel. "Nothing on earth will make me tell again."

The snake rattled his tail and laughed. "I told you secrets are hard to keep, my friend. We'll see how long you last this time."

White Pebbles

A STORY FROM ETHIOPIA

Taye was always getting into trouble.

"You need something to keep you out of mischief," said Grandpa, and he gave Taye an old gebeta board that his grandfather had made for him when *he* had been a troublesome boy.

"We can use white pebbles from the river as counters," cried Taye. "You can teach me to play."

He ran to the river and picked up some pebbles. Two merchants had set up camp there.

"Can you help us?" one asked Taye. "We need wood for our fire — we can't find any more."

"This is wood," said Taye, holding up the gebeta board.

"So it is," said the other merchant. He snatched the gebeta board and thrust it into the fire.

"That was my grandpa's," cried Taye.

"Sorry, I had no idea," the merchant said. He handed Taye a knife with a beautifully carved handle. "Here, take this instead."

A real knife for a gebeta board! A tool instead of a toy! Taye thrust it into his belt and set off. Just wait until he showed Grandpa!

"Hey, little one. May I borrow your knife?"

Taye looked up to see a farmer in the branches of a tree. "Why do you need it?"

"To cut back this tree."

Taye stood on tiptoe to hand over the knife. "Be careful. I've only just got it."

The farmer started hacking away. Almost at once, the blade snapped on the hard wood. Taye was most upset.

120

"Please forgive my clumsiness," said the farmer. "Here, have this spear instead."

A spear for a knife! A hunter's weapon instead of a tool! Taye held the spear over his shoulder, pretending he was a warrior. Just wait until he showed Grandpa!

A hunter hushed Taye from behind a bush. "Don't make so much noise, little boy."

"What are you trying to catch, hunter?"

"A lion. But I have lost my spear. May I borrow yours?"

"Be careful with it," said Taye, giving him the weapon.

The man hooted like an owl and suddenly many hunters stepped out from the shadows and disappeared among the trees, silent on bare feet. A moment later, Taye heard a roar and a shout.

"Have you caught the beast?" he asked the hunter, when he emerged from the woods.

"Yes, but I lost your spear."

Taye wanted to kick the hunter. He hadn't even shown it to Grandpa yet.

"Do not cry, little boy," said the hunter. "Take my donkey instead."

A donkey for a spear! A real live animal instead of a weapon! Grandpa would be so pleased. Taye led the donkey along the road. He would be home soon, just in time for supper.

An old woman was on her way home from the market, a huge bundle on her back. "Hey, son," she called. "May I ride your donkey? My load is too heavy to carry."

"Be gentle with him," said Taye. "I've only just got him."

The old woman struggled to climb onto the donkey's back. She poked him with her sharp toenail and the donkey brayed and bolted. Taye chased him but he disappeared over the hill.

"I'm sorry, little boy," said the old woman. "Here, take this token of my regret." And she dug into her enormous bundle and pulled out a gebeta board.

"What luck," beamed Taye. "It's like I never lost mine in the first place."

"What kept you so long?" asked Grandpa when he got home.

"White pebbles are hard to find, Grandpa," said Taye, digging them out of his pockets.

Grandpa started placing the pebbles around the board. "Now watch carefully. You need to use your brains if you want to win at gebeta."

And Taye settled down to learn.

Dinner for All

A STORY FROM SOMALIA

It was a lean time in the grasslands. The animals were hungry. A lion, a crocodile, a hyena and a leopard teamed up to hunt together, and caught a gazelle for their dinner.

"Who's going to divide the meat?" asked Lion. He hadn't eaten for a week and was ravenous.

"Someone who would do it fairly," said Crocodile.

"But of course," said Lion. "Hyena should do the honours."

Hyena cut the carcass into two equal parts. "One half for the king of the grasslands," she said, "the other half to be shared between all the others."

"What?" The lion swiped at the hyena with his enormous paw, ripping her hind leg. "Do you call that fair? I worked harder to get us this food than anyone else. Leopard, you divide the kill."

Leopard pushed one half of the carcass towards Lion. "One half for the king, as Hyena said, and one half to be divided between everyone here."

When the lion had eaten his share, Leopard cut the rest of the meat in two again. "One half for Lion, the other half to be enjoyed by everyone assembled here."

"That's fair," smirked Lion, gobbling up the second piece of meat.

Leopard divided the rest of the meat in two again. "One half for Lion, the other half for all who took part in the hunt . . . " And so it went on, with Leopard dividing the meat into smaller and smaller bits, until there was only a small mouthful left for the animals to eat.

Lion smacked his lips with satisfaction. "That was a good meal," he laughed. "But tell me, Leopard, who taught you to divide meat so fairly?"

Leopard spoke so softly, no one was sure Lion heard the answer. "It was the thought of Hyena's injured leg, your majesty."

To this day, Hyena prowls the grasslands with a limp, but clever Leopard runs with ease.

Rain Song

A STORY FROM GHANA

The river in the jungle had shrunk to a trickle in the summer heat. The ground was completely parched, and all the animals were in despair.

"We can't live without water," wailed the warthog. "What shall we do?"

"We could move to another jungle," suggested the zebra.

"We might dig a well," said the hippopotamus.

"Don't be silly," said the snake. "All we have to do is wake up Nyame, the sky-god. He must be asleep in the sky beyond Big Mountain. If we shout loudly enough, he will wake up and send us some rain."

"I'll wake him up, then," said the lion. "I have the loudest voice in the jungle." And he tossed back his mane and started roaring, "Raah! Raah! Raah!"

The animals waited, but nothing happened. The sky remained blue. A breeze rustled the dry grass. Nyame the sky-god snored on.

"Let me have a go," said the elephant. "Nyame will definitely hear me."

She lifted her trunk and trumpeted with all her strength. "Her-eeh! Her-eeh! Her-eeh!"

The animals waited again, but still nothing happened. The leaves hung limply on the trees, without even a breeze to stir them. Nyame the sky-god snored on and on.

"I'll wake up that lazy god," cried the giraffe. "I am taller than anyone here. Nyame should hear me well enough." She stretched her long neck and started bellowing as loudly as she could. "Harumph! Harumph! Harumph!"

But, once again, nothing happened. The mosquitoes droned in the hot sunshine while Nyame the sky-god snored on and on and on.

"Let me have a go," said the monkey. "I'll climb to the top of the tallest tree. Surely the sky-god

will hear me from such a height?" She swung up a tree and started chattering. "Hee-hee! Hee-hee! Hee-hee!" Again, nothing happened. The tree frogs yawned. The sky-god snored on and on and on and on.

"I can fly," boasted the flamingo. "I'll wake up that sky-god." He soared up into the heavens and cawed: "Ha-wooo! Ha-wooo!"

But once again nothing happened. The last drop of water dried up in the river bed. The sky-god snored on and on and on and on and on.

"Can I try?" said a voice from the dried mud of the river bed. A tiny freshwater mussel was speaking, her shell shut almost completely against the fierce sun.

"How will the sky-god hear you from down there?" the snake asked.

"My children are dying of thirst," said the mussel. "I'll sing as loudly as I can."

She opened her shell a little wider and started to sing. The other animals could hardly hear her, but beyond Big Mountain, Nyame the sky-god stirred. What was that beautiful song? Was it real, or was he dreaming? Nyame craned his neck to hear better and his hair billowed across the sky, casting shade on the jungle.

The freshwater mussel kept singing. She sang about her hopes for her children and begged Nyame for rain to keep them alive. Her song was so enchanting, it brought tears to the sky-god's eyes. All at once, it started to rain. The river began to fill up. Pools of rainwater formed on the ground.

124

The animals sang and danced to celebrate. They drank till their tummies nearly burst. All around them, the leaves became plump and the flowers opened.

No one thanked the freshwater mussel, but she didn't mind. Her children were safe at last.

By Royal Command

A STORY FROM NIGERIA

Two flies were invited to the queen's annual banquet.

"Her majesty has asked the cow to look after all the animals at your table," a servant told them. "Ask her for anything you need. The queen is very anxious that all her guests enjoy themselves."

A servant brought the first course to their table: a thick pepper soup with fresh tomatoes. He served the cow and all the other animals, but left without giving any to the flies.

One of them plucked up the courage to call out, "Mrs Cow, we didn't get any food."

"The servant can't have realized anyone was sitting in those chairs," said the cow. "You are very small, you know. But, don't worry, there is plenty more food to come."

The servant struggled back to the table with the main course: dishes of stew with rice, fried plantains and roasted corn piled high on wicker trays. The flies, their tummies rumbling with hunger, couldn't wait to get stuck in. But, once again, the servant left without giving them a single morsel. The flies couldn't believe their bad luck!

"Please, don't embarrass her majesty by making a fuss," the cow advised them. "I'll make sure you get lots of pudding to make up for it."

125

When the dishes for the main course had been cleared away, the servant returned with a tray loaded with dessert plates. Each one held a special doughnut, called puff-puff. He put one in front of each animal – except the flies.

"Please, tell him to give us some dessert," the flies begged the cow.

"I'm afraid you're out of luck," said the cow, tucking into her doughnut. "The man is clean out of puff-puff."

"Do you mean there is no more food?" wailed the flies.

"If I were you, I wouldn't complain," said the cow haughtily. "You should consider yourselves lucky to have been invited at all."

What could the poor flies say? The cow was right! Being invited to the palace was a great honour, even if you did go home hungry enough to eat your own wings.

The next day, the queen was presented with a basket of palm fruit to thank her for her hospitality. Who should be dozing on it but the two flies. The queen recognized her guests straightaway. "Did you enjoy the food at the banquet yesterday?" she asked.

"We didn't get a single bite to eat," one of the flies replied. "The cow didn't help us at all. Your servant didn't see us sitting there, so we had no pepper soup, no stew, no plantains or yams and no puff-puff."

"No puff-puff?" said the queen. "That's terrible. I told Mrs Cow to look after all of the guests at your table, regardless of who they were. She should have made sure you got as much to eat as you wanted."

"She ignored all our pleas," buzzed the second fly.

"It's time we taught Mrs Cow a lesson," said the queen. "You say she ignored you? Well, from now on, you have my permission to bother her and all her family whenever you see them. That will teach her to ignore any of my loyal subjects."

The flies flew off to find the cow. And from that day on, the poor beast has never had a moment's peace. That's why cows are always swishing their tails. They are trying to get rid of the pesky flies, who persist in bothering them, by royal command.

The Rabbit's Friend

A STORY FROM KENYA

A rabbit and a hippopotamus were neighbours. The hippo often blundered into the rabbit's garden and trampled over her vegetables. At last the rabbit could stand it no longer. Her twenty children were going hungry because of the hippo's clumsiness. She decided to lure the hippo away from her land.

"I'm off to see an old friend in the jungle," she said.

"That's nice," grunted the hippo who was resting in the shade.

"My friend can do all sorts of amazing things," said the rabbit. "He has no feet but he can move faster than you or me."

"Is he a snake?" asked the hippo, shooing away flies with her tail.

"No. Snakes are cold to the touch. My friend is warm all the time, even though he has no coat."

"He must be some kind of bird, then," mused the hippo.

"Birds twitter," said the rabbit. "My friend can roar louder than you, even though he has no mouth."

"Nobody roars louder than me," scoffed the hippo.

127

"My friend does," the rabbit assured her.

"I don't believe such a creature exists," said the hippo.

"Then come with me and see for yourself," said the rabbit.

"Very well." The hippo followed the rabbit into the jungle, flattening every bush in her path. Soon the two of them came to a clearing where the branches of the trees met overhead, so that not a chink of sunlight shone through. There, blazing away within a stone circle, was a bonfire. Its eyes were two lumps of charcoal, red as rubies.

"There's my friend," said the rabbit.

The hippo, who'd never seen a flame before, stood back. "Who is he?"

"I am Fire," came the crackling reply. "Come closer, friend of my friend." The hippo tiptoed forward carefully.

"Can you feel the heat on your face?" asked the rabbit. "As I said, my friend keeps warm without a coat."

"True, but can he roar as loudly as me?"

"Listen to this," said the rabbit. She threw a dry log on the fire and the flames roared.

The hippo backed away, right to the edge of the clearing. She wasn't sure she could trust this creature who roared without a mouth and kept warm without a coat.

"He can speak and roar louder than me," she admitted nervously, "but how can he move faster than me?"

"I'll show you," said Fire mischievously, and a tongue of flame shot out across a carpet of dried twigs. Before the hippo knew it, the fire was licking at her toes.

"Ouch!" The poor beast jumped back, howling with terror. She ran for her life, crashing through bushes. When she reached the river, she dived in without hesitating. The water felt so cool on her singed toes, and her fear of meeting Fire again was so terrible, that she refused to come out ever again, and the rabbit's garden flourished ever after.

The Dancing Hyena

All the animals on the savannah were very excited because the elephants were throwing a massive midsummer party by the great lake. The hyena couldn't wait. She loved parties with live music and the chance to show off her funky dance moves.

"What time does the party start?" she asked the elephant.

"At sundown — but you aren't invited," said the elephant haughtily. "It's for animals with horns or tusks only. That means goats, antelopes, buffaloes, elephants . . . not hyenas."

The hyena couldn't believe it. Why should she miss out on a great party just because she didn't have silly things growing out of her head? She went and sat by the river on her own, feeling very sorry for herself.

The sun slid below the horizon. In the distance, the music started up and the hyena's toes began to tap. She really wanted to go to the party. It was so unfair! The hyena heaved a great big sigh.

Just then, she spotted a pair of antlers lying in the shallows, where they had been left by a deer the previous year. The hyena began to giggle. If she could stick them to her head, she would be able to go to the party after all! She hurried off and found some beeswax. She patted it on her head, then stuck the antlers to it. As she peered into the river, she could see that they looked very convincing, sticking up between her ears. In the dark, no one would be able to tell that they weren't really growing out of her head.

The hyena made straight for the party, swinging her head as she went. The elephants who were standing guard at the entrance to the party were completely fooled. They let her in, and she made straight for the ring of acacia trees that surrounded the dance floor. She was ready to party!

Round and round she went, shaking her tail in time to the music, swinging her head so that all the other guests could admire her antlers.

The moon faded and a hot African sun rose behind Mount Kilimanjaro. The hyena continued to dance on her hind legs, whirling faster and faster . . .

"Are you all right?" A concerned gazelle was talking to her, his eyes fixed on her head. "Your antlers seem to be slipping behind your ears."

"Oh!" The hyena's paws went up to the antlers. The midsummer sun was melting the beeswax.

The elephants gathered around her, trumpeting with fury.

"Those antlers aren't hers. She stole them!"

"She shouldn't be at this party!"

The hyena dropped the antlers and leapt right over the elephants' heads. In a heartbeat, she was out of the acacia circle and pelting across the plain. Only when she was on Mount Kilimanjaro did she stop. The slopes of the mountain were cool after the heat of the grasslands, so she decided to set up home there. And she never ever tried to wear antlers again!

The Sunbirds

A STORY FROM ZIMBABWE

Dzivaguru was the earth-goddess. She only had to blow her horn, and the trees would grow, the rains fall and the rivers flow. She had two pet sunbirds that brought light to the sky, but Dzivaguru preferred darkness to light, rain clouds to sunshine. Only once a year did she let the sunbirds out of their cage to bring summer warmth to the earth.

Nosenga was the son of Chikara the sky-god. He saw how dark the earth was, and he had an idea. He would bring light to the people, so they would love him instead of Dzivaguru.

Down from the sky Nosenga came, calling out to the earth-goddess. Dzivaguru did not answer. She was suspicious, and retreated to the top of a high mountain, a sunbird in each hand.

Nosenga was prepared for that move! The sunbirds were made of fire, hot to the touch, painful to hold for long. Soon Dzivaguru had to let them go and Nosenga caught them in a net. They were his now. He could control how often they flew through the heavens.

He held them up and light shone in the sky. People looked up, surprised and delighted. It was the middle of winter; they had not expected to see sunshine for a long time.

"You think you have stolen the people's love from me," Dzivaguru hissed, "but every time you hold up the golden sunbirds, I shall withhold my precious rain, so the land will dry and the crops will wilt. Show them off for too long, and the farmers will curse your name instead of bless it."

And so it has been ever since. The sun rises every day to warm the farmers' backs, helping the crops to grow. When the sunbirds stay in the sky too long, the earth is parched and people wish for cooling rains, the gift of Dzivaguru.

The Pheasant and the Hen

A STORY FROM MADAGASCAR

A long time ago the hen lived in the wild, roaming freely in the jungle. One day she ran into her old friend the pheasant.

"I'm on my way to a feast," said the pheasant. "Would you like to come?"

The hen, who was feeling peckish, accepted immediately. She followed the pheasant to the roof of a farmer's storehouse.

"I know a secret way in," the pheasant said, "and the farmer has gone to market. Follow me, and we'll have as much to eat as we want!"

The hen needed no further prompting. The birds squeezed in through a tiny gap under the eaves, to discover a store packed to the rafters with baskets of cassava, open sacks of yams and mountains of corn. The hen didn't waste any time but started munching away.

Before long, the key turned in the lock and the farmer came in. He'd come back earlier than expected. The pheasant, who'd eaten only a few grains of corn, flew up to the roof and escaped.

The hen was not so lucky. She'd stuffed herself so full, she could hardly lift her legs off the ground. The farmer caught her.

"You will pay me back for every ear of corn you stole," he said, and he locked the poor hen in a cage. Every time she laid an egg, the farmer took it to sell at the market.

The poor hen is still paying for her crime to this very day. That's why hens live in hen-houses, while pheasants roam free in the wild.

The Ostrich's Horns

A STORY FROM BOTSWANA

An ostrich bumped into a gemsbok by a dry river bed. In those days the ostrich had long, pointed horns on her head but the gemsbok had none.

"Get out of my way, you silly deer, or I'll gore you with my lovely horns," the ostrich sneered.

"Lovely? Those horns are far too big for your small head. They make you look ridiculous," the gemsbok snapped. He would have loved horns of his own and was very jealous of the ostrich.

"One more insolent word out of you and I'll run you through," the ostrich snapped.

"You'll have to catch me first." The gemsbok wasn't scared of a silly ostrich with clumsy feet!

"Are you saying you're faster than me, you four-legged ninny?" she squawked.

"I'm saying even a snail can beat a big bird like you at a race."

"You fool. I am famous all around the Kalahari desert for my speed."

"Why don't we settle the matter?" the gemsbok suggested. "Let's have a race in the river bed."

"All right," replied the ostrich, "but I cannot carry this burden on such a hot day." She took off her heavy horns and placed them on the ground.

"Horns wouldn't slow me down if I had them on my head," boasted the gemsbok.

The ostrich kicked them in his direction. "You wear them, then. Let's see how far you can go without dropping the darned things!"

The gemsbok put the horns on his head. They were heavy, but he wasn't going to admit that.

The two animals lined up and began to race. The gemsbok's hooves protected him from the sharp stones and pebbles in the river bed, but the ostrich's feet were soft and she fell behind.

"Ouch! You chose this track on purpose. Let's have another race somewhere else," she cried.

The gemsbok laughed and kept on running. He didn't want the ostrich to catch up with him because he didn't want to give the horns back, the rascal. He still has the ostrich's horns to this day!

The Cheetah's Cubs

A STORY FROM SOUTH AFRICA

A young Zulu hunter stumbled across three cheetah cubs lying under a tree. *If I trained one of them to catch antelope for me*, he thought, *I would never have to work again.*

But which cub should he take? They all looked quite fierce already, with sharp teeth and claws. In the end he took all three.

When the mother cheetah returned and found her cubs missing, she howled with rage and sorrow. Tears streamed down her face. She followed the hunter's tracks, sniffing his smell and the scent of her cubs. She tracked the little group to the hunter's hut, where he had hidden the three cubs.

"Hunter, you have broken the laws of the grassland," she called. "A man must catch his prey using strength, skill and experience, not theft."

"I ask your forgiveness," said the hunter, who was very ashamed of himself. "I have been stupid, and won't do it again." He set the cubs free and they ran to their mother, who started licking them in delight. She wanted to get the hunter's smell out of their pelt.

"Please, Mother Cheetah," said the hunter, "don't take your revenge on me. I acted out of foolishness, not cruelty."

"I shall do as you ask," she replied. "But as long as there are cheetahs in the grasslands, you shall never forget that you stole helpless cubs from their mother."

And to this day, cheetahs have a black stain running down either side of their snout. The marks remind Zulu hunters of the tears that Mother Cheetah shed for her children many moons ago.

Finders Keepers

A STORY FROM ISRAEL

A spice merchant travelled to Israel to sell his wares. He found many buyers for his spices, and made a lot of money. Having sold his last grains of spice, he was preparing to set off home when he discovered that he had lost his money-bag. Had he dropped it, or had a thief stolen it?

"I'll give anyone who finds my money-bag a just reward," he called out, hoping against hope that someone would return it.

A voice rose above the din of the crowd. "Is this your purse, sir?" A beggar in rags came forward, holding the money-bag in his hands.

"It is!" declared the merchant. "Thank you, my good man — may God bless you."

"And the reward?" piped up the beggar. "You said you'd give a just reward."

"We heard you too," said a group of shopkeepers. "The beggar is entitled to his reward."

Now that he had his money-bag back, the merchant wasn't feeling quite so generous. He made a great show of opening his money-bag and looking inside, then pulled a glum face.

"I had forty gold coins in here," he lied. "The beggar has taken twenty, so he's already had his reward."

"But I didn't even open the money-bag!" protested the beggar.

"It's true, I saw him pick it up," said a large man who was standing nearby. The crowd nodded, murmuring amongst themselves.

"You are all in this together," said the merchant. "One of you robs me and the others insist he found the money-bag on the ground and didn't open it. You are trying to trick me, just because I am a foreigner!"

"Here's a rabbi," shouted an old woman. "Let him sort the matter out."

The rabbi was happy to help. He listened first to the spice merchant and then to the beggar. Then he thought for a moment. He was sure the merchant was trying to go back on his promise to reward the finder of his money-bag.

The rabbi turned to the merchant. "You are certain that your money-bag had forty gold coins in it, sir?"

"I am," insisted the merchant.

The rabbi turned to the beggar. "But the money-bag you found had only twenty coins in it?"

"That's true," said the beggar hotly.

"That means the bag the beggar found is not the one the merchant lost," concluded the rabbi. "The merchant's bag had forty coins; this one has only twenty. The beggar can keep his find. Maybe the merchant will find his own money-bag soon!"

And the greedy merchant had to be content with that.

Three Birds

A STORY FROM SAUDI ARABIA

A tribe of Bedouin were leaving their valley in search of a new place to live. But where should they go? East or west? South across the desert, or north over the hills?

"I think we should head north," said the leader. "We may find grass for our camels and sheep there, and water in the wells."

The oldest woman of the tribe spoke through her veil. "We cannot risk moving north without knowing if it is safe to do so, and we have no time to send scouts — not human ones, anyway. They are too slow and the heat of summer will soon be upon us. With your permission, sir, I will deal with the problem . . ."

From a cage inside her tent the old woman took three birds: a pigeon, a crow and a partridge.

"Fly high, my dears," she said, setting them free one by one. "Come back and tell your grandmother what you see on the other side of the hills."

The birds were gone in an instant, swooping up into the henna-red sky. The crow was the first to return. He settled on the woman's shoulder and cawed in her ear.

"What is he saying?" asked the leader of the tribe.

"He fears it is not good country in the north," said the old woman. "There is no grass for the camels and the sheep, no prey for our dogs and falcons, no water."

"Perhaps we should head south," said the leader.

138

As he spoke, the partridge and the pigeon appeared, the pigeon cooing, the partridge gabbling.

"What are they saying?" asked the leader.

"Their report is opposite to the crow's," answered the old woman. "They say we should definitely travel north beyond the hills. The land there is lush and green. There are gazelles to hunt, water in the wells and sheltered valleys for our tents."

"Who should we believe?" the leader of the tribe wanted to know.

"Two ropes are stronger than one," said the old woman. "Let us go north over the hills."

At sunrise, the tribe dismantled their tents, rolled up their rugs and shouldered their cooking pots. The journey over the hills was long and tiring but when they pitched camp again, they had found a new home, somewhere they could prosper.

"We must thank the pigeon and the partridge for their good advice," said the leader of the tribe.

A great feast was organized, with meat and coffee spiced with cardamom and ginger. As the women sang and the children swayed, the old woman stained the pigeon's feet red, as if she were a bride getting ready for her wedding feast. She outlined the partridge's eyes with black kohl, to show she was an esteemed guest at the feast. But the crow she took from the cage and threw out into the desert. "We do not need liars in our midst," she declared.

To this very day, the pigeon wanders around on red feet and the partridge blinks eyes rimmed with black. The crow is still an outcast, living in the wilderness. The Bedouin shoo him away whenever they see him!

Precious Pearls

A STORY FROM IRAN

A jeweller once heard that a fisherman had found a pearl in his net – a blue pearl, rarer than ice in the desert, more precious than fabled silver from the moon. The jeweller knew at once that he had to have it. He packed his bags and set off across the desert, led by a guide who knew the way.

Reaching the coast safely, the jeweller managed to find the fisherman. He haggled with him, paying him far less than the pearl was worth. The jeweller laughed as he hid the pearl in a leather bag and tucked it at the bottom of his luggage. But then he started to worry. What if the guide robbed him on the way back? He could lose everything. It was far better to go alone. As long as he walked in a straight line, he would easily find his way home!

Of course, he got lost the moment he set off. For days, he wandered around in circles, weakened by hunger and maddened by thirst. He hoped to run into a spice caravan, or another traveller, but he met no one.

Eventually, the jeweller could walk no farther. He sat down on the burning sand and went

through his bag, looking for a last scrap of food that might save him from starvation. Instead, he found the little bag that contained the precious pearl. The jeweller looked at it blearily. The silly bauble was no use to him now. He drew back his arm to throw the pearl away, but just as he did, he heard a voice.

"Mister?"

Through a fog of hunger, he saw a girl approaching, her head wrapped in a sea-blue scarf, her eyes full of concern.

She held out a goatskin, dripping fresh water.

The jeweller put it to his lips and drank. Behind the girl a man appeared — her father, a Bedouin. He carried bread, pears, a melon. The jeweller did not even hesitate before he exchanged the pearl for all that food. He'd learned that there were more precious things in life than pearls!

When Dreams Come True

A STORY FROM AFGHANISTAN

A poor farmer had a dream that the djinn — magic folk — had put treasure in his house, under his bed.

"If only the djinn would make the dream come true," laughed his wife. That very same day, the farmer's dog started sniffing at something buried under the pomegranate tree.

"What is it, my dog? Have you found one of your old bones?"

But it wasn't a bone the dog had unearthed. It was a clay jar, full to the brim with silver.

"It's the work of the djinn!" exclaimed the farmer.

Then a frown clouded his face. "In my dream, I found the treasure under my bed, not under a tree."

"What's that?" someone asked from behind him. It was his neighbour, who was leaning on the fence, looking at the jar.

"A jar of treasure," the farmer explained, beginning to cover it up again. He told his neighbour about his dream. "But this is not the treasure I dreamed of. It might be bad luck to take it. I shall wait until my dream comes true."

The neighbour didn't say anything, but he made a careful note of where the jar was buried. If the farmer didn't want it, why shouldn't he take it?

That night, the neighbour returned to the farmer's field. He found the pomegranate tree and dug into the freshly turned earth, uncovering the jar. When he prised off the lid, a forked tongue flicked at his hand. The jar was full of snakes, not silver.

That farmer is plotting to kill me, thought the neighbour. *But I'll teach him not to mess with me.*

He emptied the jar through the farmer's bedroom window. The snakes, frightened of the sleeping dog, clustered under the bed for safety. In the morning, the farmer awoke to the sound of barking.

"Be quiet, dog."

He felt under the bed for his rope sandals and touched something cold and hard. A silver coin! Amazed, the farmer got down on the floor and looked. The djinn had turned the snakes under the bed into silver coins again. The farmer scooped them up into his arms. His dream had come true at last!

The Four Magicians

A STORY FROM INDIA

Four magicians decided to hold a contest to find out which one of them was the best magician, the cleverest and most powerful. Each travelled to a different part of India, collecting spells and learning magic from wise men and women along the way. After many years, they met again in the square of a remote village.

"Look what I have learned to do," said the magician who had travelled north to the snow-capped mountains. He poured bubbling liquid out of a bottle and a tiger tail appeared on the ground, complete with stripy fur.

"I can do better than that," boasted the magician who had gone east across the fertile plains. He muttered a spell from one of his many notebooks and the rest of the tiger's body appeared at the end of the tail.

"That's very impressive," laughed the third magician who had ventured south into the steamy jungle. "But watch this, brothers."

He traced a pattern with his finger on the tiger's head and the tail started to twitch. The whiskers began to tremble.

The other magicians were dumbstruck. Who would have believed that a man could bring an inanimate object to life? They turned to the fourth member of the group, wondering how he would be able to top such wizardry.

"Alas," said the fourth magician, whose name was Narendra. "I have only learned a few simple tricks that any common entertainer can do."

The other magicians smiled. Poor Narendra! He had only learned conjuring tricks!

Absorbed in their competition, they hadn't noticed that the tiger had sat up and was watching them, his tail twitching. In an instant, the tiger roared and leaped towards them.

Narendra snapped his fingers —
and a cage appeared out
of thin air, trapping it.
The third
magician held his
hands together and
bowed to him.
"Your magic is the
greatest, Narendra,
for it has saved us all
from certain death,
while mine only put us in
grave danger. Great wizardry
is not that great unless it is used with a
little bit of care and common sense. You are indeed the cleverest and most powerful magician of all."

It's Not My Fault

A STORY FROM SRI LANKA

A thief broke into a merchant's house and made off with his gold. The merchant reported the theft to the police and before long the thief was caught and put on trial.

"The people of our village are famous for their honesty," said the judge. "You have brought

great shame upon us and you will have to pay with your life."

The thief thought fast. "It's not my fault," he cried. "I was leaning against the wall of the house when it crumbled and I fell into the basement, where the gold was kept. How could I resist such temptation? If anyone is to blame, it is the builder who made such a flimsy wall."

The silly judge fell for the thief's story and sent for the builder. Realizing that he was in big trouble, the builder decided to make up a story for the judge too.

"It's not my fault the wall caved in," he pleaded. "I mixed the cement exactly as it said on the packet — two jars of powder to one of water. If it crumbled, it must be because some water leaked out of the jar. So it's the potter who made that jar who's to blame for the crime, not me."

The potter was immediately hauled before the court. He didn't know if he had sold the builder a leaky jar or not, but he wasn't taking any chances, so he too made up a story.

"I never make leaky jars, your honour," he said to the judge. "But I got distracted by a woman who asked me for directions to the goldsmith's shop while I was making the jar that I sold to the builder. So I'm not to blame. It's the goldsmith's fault for not having a bigger sign."

The foolish judge had the goldsmith brought to him and accused him of causing a woman to distract the potter who made a leaky jar that led the builder to make crumbly cement that caused the wall in the merchant's house to collapse under the weight of the thief who had no choice but to make off with the merchant's gold.

The goldsmith was even more foolish than the judge and couldn't think of a single word to say in his defence. The judge sentenced him to death.

"We can't hang the goldsmith," cried the crowd who were watching the trial. "People come from all over the country to buy his jewellery. If they stop coming, our businesses will fail."

"Someone's got to pay for the crime," insisted the judge. Then he had a brainwave. "I know, since we cannot hang the goldsmith, we'll hang the first stranger that comes to our village. That way none of us will suffer."

Word soon got out that the first traveller to set foot in the village would be hanged. So no one dared go there again — not even to buy the goldsmith's famous jewellery. Before long the villagers left in search of a better life and the village was deserted. And whose fault was that?

The Dragon Princess

A STORY FROM CHINA

A young clerk called Liu lost his job at the king's palace.

"Don't be upset," said the king's old gardener as he opened the palace gate to let him out. "Life is too precious to waste doing something you hate. You seem to be the kind of person that likes adventure. Let adventure find you!"

"What's the point in having adventure if you can't afford to eat?" Liu grumbled.

"Maybe adventure will bring you good fortune," the gardener replied, closing the gate.

Liu walked along the banks of the river, wondering where he could find shelter for the night. A girl knelt down near him to draw water for her goats. She was beautiful, the most delicate girl he had ever seen. Just looking at her made his heart beat faster in his chest. But she looked so unhappy!

"Tell me why you look sad," he said, sitting down beside her. "Maybe I can help."

The girl's green eyes filled with tears. "I doubt it," she sighed. "I am the Dragon Princess. My father rules over a magic kingdom at the bottom of a lake. He gave my hand in marriage to the Dragon Prince of this river. But instead of marrying me, the prince put a spell on me, so that I must live as a woman and herd goats. The brute was only after my dowry."

The story sounded far-fetched, but something in Liu's heart made him believe it.

"I am no warrior," he said, "but if you tell me where the evil dragon lives, I shall challenge him to a fight."

"There is a better way to rescue me," said the Dragon Princess. "Go to my father and he will break the spell, so I can return home. Then I can turn into a dragon again."

Here was an adventure! Liu listened carefully to the girl's instructions and set off, heading north to the mountains, through storms and blizzards. At last he reached the shores of a misty lake.

146

Standing under a monkey-puzzle tree, he tapped three times on the lowest branch with a stick as the Dragon Princess had instructed.

A voice called out of the mist. "Who seeks the Dragon King?"

"I bring news of his daughter," called back Liu.

The mist parted to reveal a golden path across the lake.

"Follow the path," said the voice in the water, "and you will be received."

Liu trod carefully along the path and, without knowing how, found himself in the hall of a palace. A dragon with jade-green eyes sat with his tail curled around a throne. He was surrounded by other dragons, their scales reflecting the light from thousands of lamps.

"You bring news of my daughter?" the dragon asked.

"She is under a spell," explained Liu, and he repeated everything the princess had told him.

When he finished, the Dragon King rose slowly to his feet and lifted his head. He roared so loudly that Liu had to cover his ears. Something shimmered in the middle of the room as a shape appeared out of nowhere. It was the Dragon Princess!

"My daughter. Welcome home. You are safe."

The Dragon Princess took Liu's hand. "Thank you for saving me."

The king nodded to one of his servants, who came forward lugging a huge sack filled with river pearls. "These are for you," he rumbled. "May they bring you comfort throughout your life."

Liu picked up the sack, struggling under the weight of the treasure, and in the blink of an eye, found himself standing back on the riverbank where he had met the Dragon Princess. What a fantastic adventure — and it had brought him good fortune, just as the gardener had predicted!

Evergreen

A STORY FROM MONGOLIA

In olden times the highest mountain in the world was the Humber Ula. It stood at the centre of the world. On top of that mountain grew a tree, an aspen with golden leaves. Its topmost branches reached right into the upper world, the home of the gods. From among its roots bubbled the Spring of Life. Anyone who drank its waters lived forever.

People lived in the lower world that lay below the mountain. In the warmer weather they prospered, but when the cold wind of winter tore the leaves off the trees and seeped into their bones, many died.

The wise old raven could not bear to see the people suffering like this. They had done nothing to deserve the curse that the lords of creation had placed upon them. What could he do to help them? The old raven remembered other birds talking about the Spring of Life on top of Humber Ula. Did he dare steal some of its precious water? A single drop, he knew, was enough to make all the people in the lower world immortal.

On a cold, moonless night, the raven began a long journey to the Spring of Life. The

148

mountain was high, much higher than he'd expected, and by the time he reached the Spring of Life, he was almost dead with exhaustion. The air was cold at the top of the mountain and his feathers were a mantle of ice, dragging him down.

For a moment he nestled in the aspen, huddling under its golden leaves to regain his strength. From the branch he was sitting on, he could see right through the clouds into the upper world. He knew he had to be quiet, for the lords of creation would destroy anyone who stole the Water of Life.

When he'd rested sufficiently, the raven filled his small beak with water. Then, silent as a shadow, he started on the downward journey, flitting through the night. Reaching the bottom of the mountain, he sighed with relief. He could hear the people singing around their cooking pot, beyond the forest. The warm smell of stew carried in the wind. The raven decided to swoop down and drop the Water of Life in the pot. That way, it would get into everyone's meal, and everyone would be saved.

"Whoo-whoo!" Just then, an owl swooped on a mouse. Its hunting cry startled the raven, who gasped and the Water of Life spilled out of his beak. The wind caught it and scattered it on the pine trees. The raven let out a horrified caw. His dangerous journey had been in vain!

Could he go back up the mountain again to fetch more water? No, he knew he was too old to survive such a dreadful journey again. He had missed his chance to make the people immortal. They would have to survive as best they could.

The first storms of winter shrieked through the forest, turning the last warmth of autumn to bitter cold. The trees shrank from their icy breath, dropping their leaves. Only the pines stood firm and green, undaunted by the dark season. The raven's journey had not been in vain after all. The Water of Life might not have made the people immortal but it had made the pine trees evergreen.

Big Brother, Little Brother

A STORY FROM KOREA

Two brothers owned a farm. They shared what they grew and each of them lived pretty well on it. One year, the brothers worked very hard all summer and, come the harvest, they had plenty of rice. Ten sacks each they filled, enough to see them through the winter.

When his rice was stored safely in the barn, Big Brother said to his wife, "Little Brother's family is bigger than ours. He ought to have more than us."

"Your brother is too proud to accept gifts," said Big Brother's wife. "You'll have to put a sack in his store without telling him."

That night, Big Brother crept over to Little Brother's store with a sack of rice on his back. He left it with the others.

At breakfast the next morning, Big Brother's wife asked, "Didn't you take Little Brother the sack of rice yesterday?"

"I did," said Big Brother.

"But we still have ten sacks," insisted his wife. "I counted them myself."

Big Brother went over to the barn and counted them again. His wife was right. There were still ten sacks left. How odd!

"Why don't you give Little Brother another sack?" suggested his wife. "We can't possibly eat all that rice ourselves."

So, late that night, Big Brother slipped out again and carried another sack over to Little Brother's store.

"I don't understand it; we still have ten sacks left," said Big Brother's wife the next morning, shaking her head in bewilderment.

Big Brother turned pale. What was going on? Was a ghost playing tricks on him by

moving the rice back to his barn after he had left it in his brother's store?

A ghost in the barn! That night, Big Brother's wife placed a bowl of food near the sacks, a gift for the ghost so he would leave them alone. Her husband shouldered another sack of rice and nervously started off to Little Brother's farm.

Before long he spotted someone walking towards him, someone who seemed to be lumbering, as if he were carrying something too. Was it the ghost? As Big Brother got closer, the figure stopped and called out to him.

"Good evening, Brother. What are you doing out at this time of night?"

It was Little Brother, carrying a sack of rice on his back.

"You gave me the fright of my life!" cried Big Brother. "Where are you going?"

"I was bringing you a sack of rice," said Little Brother. "I know you've got to repair the roof of your house so I thought you might want to sell the extra rice for the money to pay for it. My wife said you're too proud to accept gifts, so I thought I'd leave it in the barn. I've given you two sacks already."

Big Brother smiled with relief. "And I put two sacks in your storeroom. My wife and I thought it was only fair as your family is bigger than ours."

"So that's why I still have ten sacks," laughed Little Brother. "I was convinced it was ghosts playing a trick on me."

"Of course there's no such thing as ghosts," said Big Brother, thinking of the bowl of food his wife had placed in their barn.

"Of course not," agreed Little Brother.

And they both set off home, Big Brother to his farm, Little Brother to his, both still carrying their sacks of rice!

The Crocodile Bridge

A STORY FROM JAPAN

Long ago, a hare wanted to travel from the island of Oki to Tokyo to see the temples, but he had no money to pay the ferryman. What could he do?

The king of the crocodiles spotted the hare sitting forlornly on the jetty, waving his long bushy tail. "Tasty," he said to himself and stuck his head out of the water. "Good evening, little rabbit."

"I am not a rabbit," snapped back the hare. "And the proper way to address me is 'Your Majesty'."

"'Your Majesty'?" laughed the crocodile. "Only a king like me is referred to as 'Your Majesty'."

"I am a king too," lied the hare, who was really the son of a lettuce farmer. "Please show some respect. I have many more subjects than you."

"That can't be true," sneered the king of the crocodiles. "There are more salt-water crocodiles in the channel between Oki and mainland Japan alone than there are hares in the whole world."

"Are there?" replied the hare. "Call them to the surface. Let's see them."

The king of the crocodiles started swishing his tail, which was his way of calling his subjects, and in less time than it takes a dentist to pull out a rotten tooth, the sea was teeming with crocodiles, all baring their teeth. There were so many of them, the hare couldn't see a single drop of water between Oki and the mainland.

"I still say there are more hares in the world than crocodiles," he said firmly.

"Impossible!" roared the king of the crocodiles.

"There's only one way to settle it," declared the hare. "We'll have to count all our subjects and see who wins."

"Go ahead and count," said the king of the crocodiles. "I'm tired of arguing."

"I can count much quicker if your subjects form an orderly line," suggested the hare. "That way we'll be sure not to leave any out."

The king snarled an order and the crocodiles hastily joined together, side by side, all the way from Oki to mainland Japan. The hare hopped on to the back of the first one and started counting. "One, two, three, four . . ."

Before the king of the crocodiles realized he'd been tricked, the hare had crossed the channel on the backs of the crocodiles and was safely on the mainland.

"Why, you're not a king at all!" he howled.

"No," said the hare cheekily, "but I am obviously cleverer than you. Thank you for building me a bridge."

The king of the crocodiles snapped at him but he only managed to bite off his long bushy tail. The hare laughed and set off for Tokyo to see the temples.

Ever since then, hares have always had a short tail.

The Parrot's Problem

A STORY FROM THAILAND

A farmer stole one of his neighbour's chickens. When he'd cooked and eaten it, he threw the bones in the river.

That evening, his neighbour came round for a glass of tea. "One of my chickens is missing," he said, sitting on the farmer's porch.

"Perhaps it wandered off into the woods," suggested the farmer.

"It's never strayed from the yard before."

The farmer touched an amulet on his arm. "Perhaps the tree ghosts kidnapped it. There are lots of ghosts in the woods."

"Don't blame the ghosts," piped up a shrill voice. "You stole the chicken and dumped the bones in the river."

The farmer glared at a cage that was hanging beside him. "Shut your beak, you silly parrot."

"I saw everything," insisted the parrot.

"Your eyes played tricks on you," growled the farmer. "What I cooked was a piece of meat I bought at the market."

"Hold on," said the neighbour, getting to his feet, "your parrot has never lied before. Everyone knows that parrots speak their mind. He must be telling the truth."

The matter went to court, and the parrot was scheduled to be a witness – the only one. The farmer was worried. If the judge believed the parrot, he would be in real trouble. So the wily farmer came up with a plan. The night before the hearing, he threw a piece of cloth over the parrot's cage. Then he started playing his drum, making it sound like thunder rolling in the distance. He poured water over the cage through a sieve, soaking the bird.

"What a terrible storm," sniffled the parrot, shaking the water out of his feathers. "I wish the farmer would take me indoors."

At court the next day, the judge summoned the parrot to the witness box. An official brought in his cage.

"Is it true that your owner stole the neighbour's chicken?" the judge asked.

"Yes," said the parrot. "He cooked and ate it. I saw him do it."

Everyone in the crowded courtroom gasped. The farmer was sure to be found guilty now.

"Your honour," said the farmer, "you cannot rely on my parrot to give truthful evidence. He is an unreliable witness."

"But you have always boasted that your parrot tells the truth," the neighbour shouted, cutting in.

"I wish it were so," said the farmer, shaking his head. "But my parrot is always making things up. He tells really big lies every now and then. Go on, ask him what kind of weather we had last night."

"Very well," said the judge. "I shall ask, in the interests of fairness." He fixed the parrot with a serious look. "What kind of weather did we have last night?"

"There was a terrible storm," said the parrot straight away. "The thunder woke me up. I was soaked through by the time the rain stopped."

Everyone in the courtroom gasped again. The previous night had been clear and warm, with not a hint of thunder.

"You see?" shouted the farmer. "You cannot rely on a parrot for evidence!"

"You're right," said the judge. "I can't believe a word that this parrot says, so there is no evidence against you."

The judge dismissed the case and the farmer went home a happy man. But he still had some unfinished business with his annoying pet!

Late that night, the farmer took the parrot to the deepest part of the woods. "See how you like it out here with the ghosts and the snakes, you traitor," he said, shaking the poor bird out of the cage. "I won't look after you any more."

The poor parrot found life very hard in the woods. He had to find his own food, and he had nowhere to shelter any more. How he wished he was safe in his cage!

Other parrots heard what had happened to the truthful parrot and decided to change their ways. Ever since then, parrots don't dare to speak their minds. Instead, they repeat what their owners say over and over again, to make sure they never get into trouble by contradicting them!

Food for the Emperor

A Vietnamese emperor had three sons. They were all handsome, gifted and hugely talented in their own way. But which one of them was fit to inherit the crown when he retired?

The emperor summoned his three sons. "I want each of you to prepare a meal for the New Year festival. He whose food pleases me the most will become emperor after me."

The three sons went to work at once. The eldest left Vietnam, travelling abroad in search of exotic ingredients. He knew that his father liked fine cuisine, so nothing but the rarest and most interesting food would do.

The second prince hired the best cookery teachers in Vietnam. He would learn to cook his father's favourite dishes – only he would make them even more delicious than the ones the emperor had tasted before.

The third son, whose name was Tiet Lieu, journeyed only as far as the paddy fields outside the city, where he harvested some rice with his own hands.

On the day of the festival, the three princes returned to the palace. They were so excited, they could hardly speak to one another. Which one of them would impress their father the most?

The eldest presented his meal first. Swordfish caught in distant seas and stuffed with a hundred different kinds of

shellfish! Skewers of delicate meat basted with fruity sauces! A giant cake shaped like a winged dragon! Who would have thought such extravagant food existed in the world? The emperor couldn't help but be amazed at his son's inventiveness.

Then the second prince served up his dishes – noodles cooked in broth to remind the emperor of his childhood, fried shrimps just like the ones served at his wedding, and a banana cake that had been the favourite of their late mother's!

The emperor was moved to tears by the dishes.

Finally, it was Prince Tiet Lieu's turn. He had made only one dish, one he had thought up himself. It was a simple rice cake mixed with bits of pork and bean paste, wrapped in green bamboo leaves. The other two princes tried not to smirk. Surely Prince Tiet Lieu would lose the contest? Why, he had used the cheapest of ingredients, ones that could be found at any farmers' market in the land.

The emperor finished eating and sat on the throne to pass judgement.

"I was very impressed with your meal," he said to the eldest prince. "You showed a lot of drive and ambition by gathering so many exotic ingredients and cooking them in such an original way."

Then he addressed the second prince. "I found your meal very comforting. A lot of thought was put into choosing the dishes so close to my heart. You have done well!"

At last he turned to Prince Tiet Lieu. "Your dish was simple and easy to make. The ingredients are so cheap, the poorest people in the empire can afford them. It gives me great joy to know that every one of my subjects can eat such satisfying and nourishing food. I liked the shape of the cake too. It reminded of me the fields in which our farmers toil; the green wrapping made me think of the harvest. Well done, Prince Tiet Lieu. Your dishes have shown me that you are thoughtful and sensitive to the needs of our people. You, therefore, will inherit my empire."

Prince Tiet Lieu became the emperor and his rice cakes proved so popular that Vietnamese people still make them for the New Year festival to this very day.

A Birthday Surprise

A STORY FROM THE PHILIPPINES

It was Irma's ninetieth birthday and she was in a bad mood.

"I wish I had something really nice to eat today," she grumbled to her husband, Miguel. "And wouldn't it be nice if I could afford to repair the leaks in the roof, and had a child to look after? Grown-ups should have children around the house to keep them young. We have nothing and no one."

Miguel wandered outside into the street to get away from his complaining wife. Almost immediately he came back with a pumpkin under one arm. "Look what I found outside the door, Irma. Who do you suppose left it there?"

"Who cares where it came from? That's one of my birthday wishes come true," Irma said, clapping her hands with glee. Now she had something delicious to eat.

She sliced the top off the pumpkin and there inside it was a little baby with golden eyes, his knees tucked tightly under his chin.

That was her second birthday wish come true!

Irma set a wooden tub on the table, fetched the soap, and started giving the baby a bath, to wash off the pumpkin seeds. But how amazing! Every drop of water that touched

the child turned into a golden coin. Soon the tub was full to the brim with treasure. Irma couldn't believe her eyes. "Miguel, come and see," she called. "That's another of my wishes come true. Perhaps there is something magical about turning ninety that means I'm getting everything that I wished for."

She sent Miguel to buy a birthday cake, and to hire a roofer. While he was gone, she started thinking. Why settle for repairing the roof of an old house when, with enough gold, she could buy herself a new palace? Why be content with just a birthday cake, when she might be able to afford a banquet every night?

Quickly, Irma filled the tub with water again. If she washed the baby again, she could get even more gold.

"The poor mite doesn't need another bath," said Miguel, coming back with the cake. "He's as clean as a whistle already."

Irma didn't even hear him. She picked up the baby and lowered him into the water. This time, gold spilled out of the tub and all over the floor.

"Fetch more water, Miguel!" cried Irma. "Hurry! Hurry! There's no time to waste. We must bathe him again!"

"But what are we going to do with all this gold?" protested Miguel. "We are old, Irma. We have enough here to last us the rest of our lives already."

Just then the poor little baby sneezed. Soap had got up his nose and into his eyes. A moment later he vanished, just like that! And all the gold in the tub and on the floor turned back into soapy water. The kitchen was flooded and Irma was left with just a puddle and a pumpkin.

Poor woman! Her birthday wishes had come true but her greed had ruined everything. She spent the rest of the year hoping there was something magical about turning ninety-one as well, so she could have another go!

The Secret in the Parcel

A young pilgrim journeyed barefoot for many days and nights to beg a favour of a holy man who lived alone in a mountain cave.

"Oh father of the poor, help me," he implored, kneeling at the holy man's feet.

"What do you need, my son?" the holy man asked.

"All my life I have thought only of myself, great father. Now I want to help others."

The holy man handed the young pilgrim a small parcel wrapped up in banana leaves.

"Take this."

"What's in it, father?"

The holy man smiled, wrinkling his ancient blue eyes. "A gift. But take care that you do not unwrap it before the moon comes up, or you will release a power that not even I can control."

"Thank you, father." The pilgrim kissed the holy man's hands, put on his sandals and started on the long journey home. It was midday when he reached the jungle at the foot of the mountain, a long time before moonrise.

I wonder what's in the parcel, he thought. He pressed his fingers all over the banana leaves but he couldn't feel anything. Whatever the contents of the mysterious parcel were, they had to be very small.

Perhaps I'm carrying a diamond, thought the pilgrim, *or a ruby. No — it can't be a jewel. The holy man said it was something powerful.*

What was it, then? The young pilgrim couldn't take another step along the path before he found out what he was carrying. He decided to have a peep in the package — as the holy man had known he would.

He strayed off the path into the forest so no one would see him. It was dark as night under

161

the trees; not a chink of sunlight filtered through the branches overhead. The pilgrim peeled away layers of banana leaves with trembling hands. The parcel got smaller and smaller, till it was no bigger than a fist, then a marble, then a pea.

Inside the final layer of leaves was a seed. Just a seed and nothing more!

The pilgrim had expected something dazzling, something out-of-this-world. A magical ring perhaps, or an amulet. Not a seed. What was so special or powerful about a seed? Farmers scattered seeds on the ground all the time. They fed them to birds.

The pilgrim had seen people nibble on seeds too. Perhaps he should eat this seed. He hadn't had any food since he left the holy man's cave at dawn and he was ravenous. The seed was tiny, but it might take the edge off his hunger. *That will teach the great father to trick me*, the pilgrim thought bitterly.

He popped the seed onto his tongue and swallowed it. Instantly, he felt a searing pain in his stomach and bent over, clutching his sides. His feet sank into the ground, burrowing deep into the soil. His hands flew up, reaching towards the sky, growing longer and longer, parting the branches of the forest canopy . . .

Later in the day, some women came looking for food. In the spot where the pilgrim had been, they found a strange tree they had never seen before. Strange round fruit with a hard shell was dangling from its branches, waiting to be picked. The women climbed up and plucked a couple of them. They broke them open using a heavy stone, and marvelled at the sweet milk and white flesh within. The women were delighted. Here was something they could feed their hungry families!

The holy man had answered the pilgrim's prayer after all. The magic seed had turned the pilgrim into the first coconut tree in the world. His descendants are still helping people to fill their hungry stomachs to this very day.

Clever Friends

A STORY FROM INDONESIA

Guno and Koyo shared a farm. Guno was in charge of the rice field. Koyo looked after the cattle. One summer Koyo said, "Let's dig a well, so I don't have to keep going down to the river every time I need some water."

When the two friends had finished digging, Koyo said, "Look, we've left a big mound of earth in the field. We can't leave it there. Snakes might make their nests in it."

"We can't encourage snakes to live on our farm," agreed Guno. "But how can we get rid of all this earth?"

Koyo scratched his head. "I know," he said. "Let's dig a hole in the ground and bury it."

The two of them set to with their spades again, throwing the earth behind them as they dug. They didn't stop until they'd made a pit deep enough to take all the earth from the well.

"There!" said Koyo. "Problem solved." He turned to put away his spade and saw the pile of earth they'd dug out of the second hole.

"Don't worry," laughed Guno. "We'll get rid of it in exactly the same way we dealt with the first pile of earth."

It took them most of the next day to dig another hole. By the time they'd put in all the earth from the previous hole, they were feeling pretty sore and thirsty.

"Let's go to town and celebrate," suggested Koyo.

"We can't celebrate yet, I'm afraid," said Guno, and he turned Koyo around to show him another gigantic mound of earth behind him.

"Bother," grunted Koyo. "Why does this keep happening? Every time we solve one problem, another one rises up to take its place. I'm tired of digging holes. Where can we put this mound of earth?"

"Can't we put it down the well?" asked Guno. "The snakes might not find it there."

Both men started shovelling as fast they could and before sunset they had filled in the well. Not a trace of dug-up earth remained in the field.

"Problem solved," declared Guno. "Aren't we clever?"

"Aren't we just?" agreed Koyo, and he saddled the donkey for a trip to town.

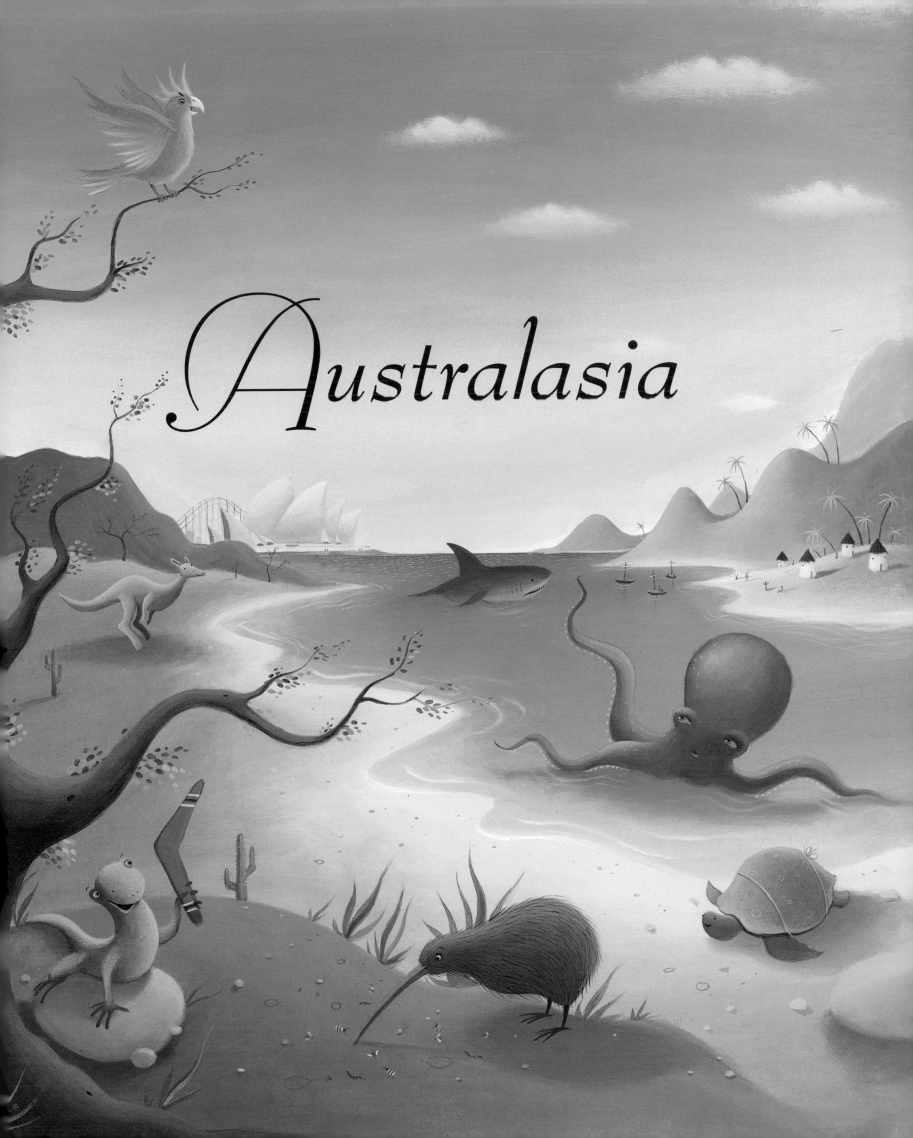

Australasia

Boomerang

A STORY FROM AUSTRALIA

It was hot, hot, hot and Oolah the young lizard was practising with his boomerang, throwing it as far as possible. He and his mates were having a contest soon, and Oolah wanted to be sure to win!

"Be careful, you nearly hit me!" complained Galah the cockatoo from the branches of a eucalyptus tree.

"It's not my fault you decided to sit up there, old lady," replied Oolah rudely. "Why don't you go and have a snooze somewhere else?"

Young creatures nowadays, the cockatoo fumed. They had no respect and no manners. "I'm not an old lady and I am certainly not having a snooze," she snapped, ruffling up her feathers and shaking out her wings. "I'm sitting on my eggs like a good cockatoo mother should."

Old people! thought Oolah. They were always making a fuss, as if whatever they did was important, but whatever he did wasn't. He threw his boomerang again, as hard as he could, and this time it passed so close to Galah, it shaved the feathers clean off the top of her head. Only a few remained, sticking up like plumed reeds in the river.

"You nearly killed me, you insolent rascal!" screeched Galah. "I'm going to teach you a lesson."

Oh dear! It was said in the bush that Galah knew some powerful magic. She was also known to be vicious when she was upset. Oolah dropped his precious boomerang and bolted. Even if there was no truth in the rumour about Galah's magical ability, he didn't want her to sink that famously sharp beak and those razor-sharp claws into him. But the cockatoo was faster than the lizard had expected. She swooped down, caught Oolah in her surprisingly large claws and hurled him into a bindeah bush.

Poor Oolah! The bindeah bush was covered in spikes which got stuck to his back.

"I put a spell on you," snarled Galah, flapping around the bush. "You will remain prickly forever more. That'll teach you to be rude to your elders and neighbours."

"And I put a spell on you too," groaned Oolah, who knew a little magic of his own. "As long as I remain prickly, you shall only have a small tuft of feathers on your head. Everyone will be able to see where my boomerang hit you."

Both Galah's spell and Oolah's spell came true. Moloch lizards in Australia continue to have a prickly back, while cockatoos are always trying to slick down a tuft of feathers on their head.

The Kiwi's Gift

A STORY FROM NEW ZEALAND

Insects were demolishing the great forest, feasting on the trees, chomping through the branches until they fell to the leaf-littered floor. Tanemahuta, the god and guardian of the forest, was very concerned.

"I shall give you one of my birds to protect the forest," said the god's brother, Tanehokahoka. He was the lord of the birds, the protector of everything that flew in the air. "The bird and his family will live on insects to lessen their numbers."

Tanehokahoka called out to all the birds, and they came flapping to the high rock, jostling to find a spot close to their god at the top of the Kauri tree, the highest perch in the forest.

"The forest needs urgent help," explained Tanehokahoka when all had settled in the branches. "The trees are being eaten alive by insects. I want one of you to move your family to the forest floor, to keep their numbers in check."

His request was greeted with silence. Move to the forest floor where it was dark, and hungry animals prowled? All the birds shuddered at the very thought. They were created to fly in the sun, to flee from danger into the sky.

"I know it's a big sacrifice," said Tanemahuta, "but my brother assures me that one of you will offer themselves." He fixed his night-dark eyes on the blue-feathered Tui bird, who was sitting right at his feet. "Will you move to the forest floor, Tui?"

168

The bird did not dare look into the god's eye as he shook his head. "You know I am scared of the dark. I hear the sun never shines through the canopy."

Tanemahuta turned to Pukeko, the little hen. "Will you consider moving?"

"They tell me the forest floor is littered with rotting leaves," cried Pukeko. "The damp will ruin my dainty feet."

"How about you, Pipiwharauroa? Will you give up the sunshine to protect the trees?"

The shining-cuckoo stared at his feet. "I am too busy building a new nest in the Cabbage Tree. My wife is expecting to lay eggs soon."

"I see," said Tanemahuta quietly.

Just then, the kiwi flapped his enormous rainbow-wings. "I will move."

All the other birds gaped in astonishment. The kiwi liked nothing better than soaring through the sky on his great wings, riding the wind. Why would he choose to spend the rest of his life on the forest floor?

"If the forest dies," said the kiwi, "we shall all lose our homes. We will all perish. I do not want that to happen to my children, or any other bird's children for that matter."

"I must warn you," said Tanemahuta gently, "that once you give your word, once you move to my kingdom, you will not be able to return to the realm of the air. You will lose your ability to fly forever."

"I understand," said the kiwi bravely, trying to keep the fear out of his voice. He took one last look at the dazzling sunshine and the bright blue sky. Then he climbed down through the forest canopy. The branches of the trees closed over him, hiding him from view.

"Your lack of courage disappoints me," Tanehokahoka cawed at the birds left on the Kauri tree. He pointed his beak at the three closest to him, the ones that always made sure they were at the front of the crowd. "From now on, Tui Bird, you shall have two white feathers on your neck, a badge to show that you are cowardly. And you, Pukeko, with your airs and graces, you shall live forever in the marshes where your feet shall always be covered in mud. As for you, Shining-Cuckoo, you will never build another nest, but lay your eggs in other birds' homes."

He looked down through the trees where the brave kiwi was starting to gobble up insects by the beakful. "As for the kiwi, his feathers will lose their beautiful colours because he lives in the shade. His wings will grow so small they will practically vanish, but he will be one of the most respected birds in the world, a shining example of selfless love and bravery. He will always be associated with the true spirit of this wonderful land."

And Tanehokahoka's words came to pass — to this day, a small, flightless bird no larger than a hen is one of the most famous in the world!

The Turtle's Shell

A STORY FROM PAPUA NEW GUINEA

Wagtail was on his way to Hornbill's summer party. All the birds were invited! They would dance and sing and make merry for days. But what did Wagtail spy as he flew over Hornbill's orchard? What was scurrying about, dodging slyly from tree to tree? Why, it was Turtle, pilfering mangoes.

"Stop, thief! Stop!" Wagtail chirped.

Other birds swooped up to help catch the thief. Hornbill was the most powerful bird in the rainforest, and they all wanted to impress him.

In those days Turtle did not have a shell on his back, so the sight of all those sharp beaks bearing down on him terrified him. He started running. Poor Turtle! Stumpy legs are no match for feathered wings. Before he'd even reached the orchard gate, he was surrounded by screeching, squawking, pecking birds. They trussed him up with creepers and dragged him, struggling and squirming, in front of Hornbill.

The great bird glared at Turtle with beady eyes. "Take the thief to the other end of the orchard. I don't want to see his sorry face while I'm eating. We'll deal with him after the feast. He'll be our evening entertainment!"

The birds dragged Turtle to the other end of the orchard and lashed him to a tree. The poor thing hadn't eaten anything but a couple of mangoes all day and the smell of food on the fire made his mouth water.

He was not alone in his hunger. Three young hornbills were peeping through the trees, eager to catch a glimpse of the party.

"I think they've put the plantains to roast on the fire."

"Wish we could have some."

"They're having guavas and mangoes too."

Turtle smiled at the little birds.

"Doesn't your papa want you to go to the feast?"

"No, he says we're too young. The summer celebration is for grown-ups only. We must stay out of the way until the dancing is over."

"That doesn't sound fair," said Turtle.

"They are having drummers too," sighed one of the young hornbills. "But we won't be able to see them from here."

"You like dancing, I take it?" asked the turtle.

"We do. All three of us."

"I'm considered a very good dancer, even if I say so myself," said the turtle. "In fact, I teach all the little turtles to dance."

The young hornbills looked him up and down. The turtle seemed a bit too old – a bit too plump – to be a dancer. "Do you?"

"Untie me, and I'll show you a great dance."

The little hornbills looked at each other. Papa was feasting at the other end of the orchard – he would never find out what they had done. Eagerly, they pecked at the creepers with their beaks until they lay in shreds on the floor.

"Go on, Mr Turtle. Teach us a dance."

The turtle thought for a second. He'd tricked the young hornbills into freeing him, but he still had to venture past the party if he wanted to escape. And that meant facing those birds' razor-like beaks and claws again. He'd need suitable protection.

"We can't dance without dressing up," he said to the young hornbills. "It wouldn't be any fun."

"Oh, but we have no costumes. What shall we do?"

"Make our own, of course. We could use all sorts of things."

The young hornbills looked around them. "What sort of things?"

"Anything! That big gourd on the ground over there, for example. Tie it to my back and it will look like a warrior's shield."

The hornbills flapped their wings with joy. "Oh yes, a warrior's shield. How clever."

They used the remains of the creepers to secure the gourd to the turtle's back. The turtle started dancing, whirling on two feet, clapping his front legs together, winking and grinning. Then he made a dash for it.

It took only a moment for the young hornbills to realize they'd been tricked. "Dad! Dad! Turtle has escaped!"

Hearing their screeching, Hornbill looked up from his food and squawked an order. A cloud of angry birds took to the air, fanning out over the orchard like a raincloud heavy with storm. Wagtail spied Turtle running among the guava trees.

"There he is! There's the thief!"

Once more, snapping beaks and raking claws descended on Turtle. But this time he was not such easy prey. This time his back was covered. Sweating in the summer heat, Turtle made it safely out of the orchard to the shore beyond. He plunged beneath the waves, out of the birds' reach.

The birds squawked angrily. They'd never seen Turtle in the ocean before; they'd never expected him to dive into the water. And now he'd given them the slip! But wait until he came back to land — then they'd show him.

Deep beneath the waves, Turtle stretched his tired legs. He felt weightless in the water, as if he were young again. The water felt cool on his skin. He decided to make the ocean his home. And he never took the gourd off his back either. It was the perfect armour against hungry beasts.

That's why, even today, turtles wear a thick protective shell on their back.

Beware of the Shark!

A STORY FROM FIJI

Dakuwaqa was the god of the sea, the guardian of the islands of Fiji. Half-man, half-shark, he loved nothing better than roaming the sea, especially if he could pick fights with other gods and challenge them to battles along the way.

One day, speeding through the clear waters around the island of Yanuca, he met another shark-god, Masilaca.

"Where are you going, brother?"

"To make mischief!"

"You are not going to Kadavu Island, I hope," said Masilaca, who was slightly jealous of Dakuwaqa. "I hear the guardian spirit of that island has never lost a battle."

Those words were practically an invitation to Dakuwaqa.

"Yes, I am going to Kadavu Island. I feel like causing mischief inland today, not just in the sea. So I am going to swim upriver."

"Kadavu's guardian spirit is very powerful, my friend. She will not let you harm her people."

"I have fought and humiliated many other gods and guardian spirits," laughed Dakuwaqa. "I am afraid of no one. The protector of Kadavu Island will be one more shell in my necklace of victories."

Masilaca bared his teeth in a false grin. "Then great speed and strength to you, my brother."

It didn't take Dakuwaqa very long to reach Kadavu. Tiny movements in the water told him that fishermen were casting nets and divers were searching for pearls in the mouth of the river. Perhaps he could nibble on a few of them before going further inland. He was hungry. So much for that infamous protector of Kadavu . . .

Suddenly Dakuwaqa found himself enveloped in thick, velvety darkness. He coughed on ink.

The spirit guardian of Kadavu had arrived and she was an octopus!

Her voice boomed out of the depths. "Turn back, oh slayer of people."

The shark-god opened his mouth to reveal banks of well-honed teeth. "Dakuwaqa does not tremble in front of an octopus, even a giant one."

"Continue at your peril, then."

Dakuwaqa gathered speed, trying to move forward. But something in the darkness was blocking his way. The octopus had stretched her giant tentacles across the entire inlet.

The shark gnashed his teeth in fury, trying to bite into the octopus's flesh. It was no use.

The giant octopus's skin was too hard. She wrapped her tentacles around him and started to squeeze, hard. Dakuwaqa tried to wriggle out of her grasp, thrashing his tail and fins, but the octopus's powerful suckers held him fast. For the first time in his life, the god of the sea started to panic. Sharks die if they stop swimming.

"I concede defeat. Release me, I beg you."

"Only if you promise to leave the people of Kadavu alone."

"I will do more than that. I will protect them wherever they go," Dakuwaqa promised.

"Then you are spared."

The giant tentacles released their hold on the shark, snaking out of sight in the ink-stained water. Two great eyes, bright with triumph, glared at Dakuwaqa from the depths.

"Hail Dakuwaqa, protector of all Fiji."

"Hail, noble protector of Kadavu."

With those words, Dakuwaqa turned and sped away, his body humming with pain, his mind agonized with the humiliation of his first defeat. Since then he has not harmed anyone from Kadavu, no matter how far from home he has found them. If you ever go to that paradise island yourself, you will see people swimming fearlessly among the sharks. True to his word, Dakuwaqa is still protecting them from harm today.